A Sweet Deal

MONICA TILLERY

Author of *Adam's Ambition* and *Kiss Me, Katie*

CRIMSON
ROMANCE
F+W Media, Inc.

Published by
Crimson Romance
an imprint of F+W Media, Inc.
10151 Carver Road, Suite 200
Blue Ash, OH 45242. U.S.A.
www.crimsonromance.com

ISBN 10: 1-4405-8070-7
ISBN 13: 978-1-4405-8070-3
eISBN 10: 1-4405-8071-5
eISBN 13: 978-1-4405-8071-0

Cover art © istockphoto.com/Piotr Marcinski

For Nitza Campos, an incredible friend and beautiful individual. I couldn't have done it without you, and I wouldn't have wanted to.

Acknowledgments

A Sweet Deal has been through many drafts, and it is a dream come true for me that it finally has a home. Without the support of my friends and, of course, my awesome husband Dave, I would have been sorely tempted to leave this story tucked into my hard drive.

Thank you to my favorite early readers, Nitza Campos, Christine Grazioli, Amy Valentine, and Rachel Sweigart. I appreciate your enthusiasm and support for this project; your feedback helped shape what it finally became, and I doubt it would've ever seen the light of day without your help!

Thank you so much to Nitza Campos, who lent me her middle and maiden names, suggested outfits for Yvette, braved her parents' wrath to check for authenticity in my writing, and shared everything about Puerto Rican cooking with me. There is no Yvette without you!

My huge thanks also to Leslie McKinney, my beautiful friend, for sharing your story of what it's like to have cancer as a teen. Thank you for letting me shamelessly use your experiences.

Finally, I am supremely grateful for my amazing editor, Tara Gelsomino. I love working with you and appreciate the work you put into this project. It definitely wouldn't have been the same without you. As always, I would love to do it again!

Chapter One

Richard slipped into the conference room and raised his eyebrows at his father, who waved at him to keep quiet and take a seat. One more meeting and he'd be out of the office until after the big Confectioners Association conference. Throaty laughter floated through the speaker, catching his attention and making him wonder who was on the line.

"Have you reviewed the offer? You should've received the most current information last week."

His father sat forward on his elbows and spoke into the phone. "Yes, ma'am. I've been going over the details, but I still need to meet with my son. I want him to have a clear view of what's on the table before we make any big decisions. He's going to be the one taking over when I retire." His father leaned back in his chair, a mischievous twinkle in his eye. "Of course, if he won't agree, maybe I'll just say yes so we get to spend more time together." He grinned at Richard, clearly pleased with his little joke, which only managed to set his son's teeth on edge.

"Michael, you are too much." A sexy, feminine voice wound through the conference room, smooth as melted cocoa butter and twice as decadent. "You've got to let me buy you a drink in Vegas so we can hash this out. I know you'll see things my way."

"I'd love that, Yvette, but I'm buying. I insist."

Yvette? It must be Yvette Cruz, the mergers and acquisitions representative from Saffron Sweets. The one who'd been approaching his father from every angle to convince him to agree to a buyout.

More than thirty years ago, Michael Morgan had started the family business at the urging of Richard's mother, Amelia, a fabulous cook with an unquenchable sweet tooth. The neighborhood candy shop in a quiet section of Philadelphia was an immediate success, and Richard and his brother Robert grew up amid its gleaming confectionary jars, sweeping and dusting, manning the cash register, and serving customers. They'd even assisted their mother with recipes for new confections.

The business grew rapidly during the past three decades from a thriving regional brand to a national conglomerate—all the while remaining family owned and privately held. Newer, bigger divisions arose that supplied beverages, pet care products, and household chemicals to consumers, and now Morgan Enterprises was one of the largest privately-held companies in the country with divisions spread across America.

However, with the new directions, confections had faltered and consistently lost money over the last several quarters. Selling it to Saffron Sweets, a startup chocolatier that had traded artisanship for mass-production and reaped considerable profits and growth over the last few years, made good business sense.

His father was relaxed, with a fond smile on his face, and a playful tone that matched hers in his voice. This woman represented the death of the one thing in the world Richard cared about, and his father was practically flirting with her.

"Wonderful. See you there." He could hear the smile in her voice, and it pushed his blood pressure up a few notches.

"Yep, see you soon."

They ended the call, and Richard stalked around the room, pausing to pour ice water into a crystal tumbler. He tamped down his rising irritation, unclenched his fists, and sat back down in his chair. "You already know that I don't want any division of Morgan Enterprises going public, and that includes confections. I wish you would just turn them down already. If Saffron wants to expand their product lines beyond chocolates, I don't see why they can't do that without us. I know it's not up to me, but I think this is a mistake."

He looked across the conference table at his father, who had become his mentor, his friend, and his confidante. Recently, however, they hadn't been seeing eye to eye.

"Son, I love your devotion to the company. Always have. Why you're so protective of the confections division in particular is beyond me, however. That division's been a loss leader for years, and as you know, I've been considering narrowing our focus so that pet care and chemicals gets more attention. I wouldn't mind having confections out of the picture so we can grow in other areas. Just think of how much more we could do with the profitable divisions if we shed the dead weight. It's actually lucky that they're so interested. If we sell, we can at least recoup some of our investment instead of letting confections die a slow and unprofitable death."

It never failed to surprise Richard how different their viewpoints could be despite the stubborn streak they shared. For years, that combination had kept things strained. His father had done his best, had raised Richard and his younger brother Robert with love and devotion after their mother's death, but he was busy building the business and finding the next Mrs. Morgan. He was a good father, but it wasn't until Richard was himself an adult and working with Michael in the executive offices to steer the business that they'd managed to grow closer.

"How can you say that? Candy is what made Morgan a household name! It's what we're known for, what we've always been known for. I know it isn't as lucrative as the other branches, but as a Morgan, it feels like a part of me. A part of *us*." The candy store had been his first job and his first love. For years after Amelia had passed away, Richard would visit that flagship store, convinced he could still smell her lavender perfume in the bustling kitchen.

Morgan Confectioners was a national brand, its products carried in mass retailers now, and the little Philly candy shop was long gone. Where his father saw dollars and nonexistent profit margins, Richard saw the company born from his mother's vision and hard work. Afternoons spent helping at the shop with his brother, and the time spent working as a family they'd never have again. Memories were all he had left, and he couldn't let it go without a fight. Replacing the Morgan label with Saffron's was unthinkable.

His father shook his head. "We've been over this a hundred times. Industry is about more than sentiment, son, and after I'm gone … well, you're the last Morgan in the business. I want to know that every aspect of the company is as strong as it can be. That could mean letting this one piece go for the good of the whole. I'm not sure we'll get a better offer than Saffron's, and I'd hate to see you forced into a less beneficial deal one or two years down the line."

"Dad, I'm never going to sell. I'll run everything myself once you step down in a few years. But you're still going strong, and I'm hardly the last Morgan. I'm sure Robert would come through in a crisis." He resisted the childish urge to cross his fingers on that last part. Richard's younger brother headed up his own incredibly successful record label and had no intention of ever joining the family business.

"I'm not talking about retirement; I'm talking long term here, son—our legacy," he said. "And you're the only Morgan I consider when making decisions about the company. Robert has made it very clear that he's not interested in being involved."

Richard tapped his fingers on the table and furrowed his brow. Single with no children, he could only promise to keep the company in the family as long as he lived—that much was true. They would eventually have to face the fact that Morgan could only be a family-run company as long as there were family members alive who were willing to run it.

"Richard, I know you don't want to hear this, but if you're determined to keep the business in the family, there is one other chance. It's no guarantee but it's still the best bet we've got, and I need you to consider it."

At a loss, Richard stared at his father expectantly. He'd try anything.

Michael paused for a beat and smiled, clearly amused with Richard's confusion. "You could get married."

Oh. Richard rolled his eyes and sighed. "Why does everything always come down to marriage with you?" His father loved the idea of marriage so much that he had taken the plunge two more times since the death of his beloved wife. Richard wasn't sure if the man was afraid of dying alone, trying to recreate the magic of his first fairy-tale relationship, or just in love with the idea of being in love. But it seemed that there was no limit to the chances Michael Morgan would take in his pursuit of wedded bliss.

"Don't laugh. I'm serious. A marriage means stability, children, more family. You might even like it." His father smiled kindly, the corners of his eyes crinkling.

"Because it worked out so well for me the first time?" Richard asked, his voice heavy with sarcasm.

His smile faded. "Just because it didn't work out once doesn't mean you should never try it again. I know that it's hard to believe now but not every woman is like Chelsea."

"Yes, well, thank God for that," Richard mumbled. He'd been divorced almost five years, but the lessons he'd learned still stung.

"I know. Don't you think it's been long enough, though? Do you really mean to tell me that you never want to get out there and try again? You can't let one bad experience ruin the rest of your life." His father would never truly accept that Richard was happy remaining unmarried—probably couldn't wrap his mind around it.

Richard blew out a sharp breath. "Believe it or not, I don't consider my life ruined just because I'm divorced. I'm perfectly happy concentrating on work right now, and that's all that really matters to me." Eager to move the focus away from marriage, he guided the conversation back to the acquisition. "And right now, I'm concerned. Saffron must be really serious about winning you over if Yvette's in the picture. I've heard they don't send her in unless it's critical."

Yvette Cruz was Saffron's nearly foolproof secret weapon when it came to acquiring divisions like his, and her involvement meant that things were spiraling out of his control. Rumor had it that she was beautiful, seductive, and incredibly persuasive, and knowing his father's penchant for gorgeous, younger women had Richard on high alert.

"Yvette has been in for a few meetings, yes, but you know, I'm very happy with the woman I'm seeing. She's a sharp businesswoman. She loves the new hard candies—especially the champagne lollipops—and it wouldn't hurt to strike a deal with them before they figure out that we've got nothing new coming down the pipe. They think we're a good fit for their brand, and we could push into the organic pet food market with the money we save cutting the dead weight of confections." He took a sip of water from the crystal tumbler sitting in front of him, ice tinkling against the sides.

"Dad, I don't think the confections division is dead weight. It's going through a slump, sure, but the champagne lollipops have increased interest in the brand. Once we develop something with similar impact, we'll be back in the black before we know it. I just need time. Selling to Saffron feels like giving up."

Morgan Confectioners had introduced their all-time bestselling product earlier in the year and posted their biggest sales in a decade, though it wasn't quite enough to justify the money they poured into the division. They were funneling money into research and development at unprecedented rates, trying to build on the momentum the champagne lollipops had started. Why his father couldn't see the unlimited potential ahead of them, refused to see how much a few more successful products could change things, boggled his mind.

"Well, if you're that opposed to Saffron, then you know what you have to do," his father said, a sly grin replacing the kindly smile. "If you're interested in my proposal—so to speak—then as soon as you're engaged, I will formally suspend talks of a merger with Saffron. Once you're legally married, I will turn over Morgan Confectioners to you."

Richard regarded his father and weighed the offer, considering his options. Excitement welled up at the thought of gaining outright control of Morgan Confectioners. The company was his passion, his one true love, and to have it so close, within his grasp, was a thrilling prospect.

Finding a woman who would agree to the marriage would be easy. Chelsea had proven that well enough. He'd married her for love, but it wasn't a full year before her true colors shone through. She'd been far more interested in the Morgan name and the money that went with it than with a loving marriage.

Richard had always depended on his ability to read people, to navigate situations by relying on his intuition. To have his marriage be little more than a deception rattled him terribly, landing a complete blow to his confidence. When it came to work, he always knew where he stood, what he wanted, but he doubted he'd ever be able to trust his judgment again when it came to romance.

Most of the events he attended for his charitable involvements or for business required dates, but that was as far as things went. Mentally flipping through the current selection of women he was seeing, Richard wondered if he'd actually be able go through with marrying any of them. He wouldn't do to someone else what Chelsea had done to him. No, he'd have to find a woman who stood to benefit as much as he would from the arrangement.

Or he could actually choose someone and attempt a real relationship. Right now, that was the last thing he was interested in. He'd finally reached the point after his divorce where the thought of spending time with a woman didn't turn his stomach, but there was no way in hell he was going to marry one. His marriage to Chelsea taught him one thing: he couldn't recreate the idyllic nuclear family of his childhood just because he wanted to. He'd have to figure something else out.

Richard pushed his chair back and stood as his father did the same. "Obviously I'll have to think about it, but I'll let you know what I decide. If you could hold off on making any moves with Saffron until after we return from Vegas, I would appreciate it. I'm sure Ms. Cruz will be at the conference, trying to sink her claws into you, but it will be near impossible for me to concentrate with this is on my mind."

His father straightened his jacket. "You should take a meeting with her. You might surprise yourself and actually like her. She's much less bloodthirsty than you seem to think. But of course I'll hold off on giving her an answer." He stood up. "I plan on enjoying the conference this year and hope you'll do the same. I haven't even looked at the events schedule since the packet landed on my desk, but we'll have to at least grab a drink together. See you in Las Vegas."

His father left, and Richard was alone in the opulent conference room. He slipped his hands in his pockets and looked out the window over the city skyline, the possibilities spreading out before him. Michael's somewhat indecent proposal would have to wait. The National Confectioners Association Conference was being held in Las Vegas this weekend, and it was the biggest, most important industry event of the year. Vegas was one of Richard's favorite cities in the world and he was looking forward to the conference even more than usual this year. With any luck, he'd make the necessary appearances and still have plenty of time to hit the casino. A little harmless gambling was just what he needed. It was good to be on top, and Richard intended to enjoy every moment of the conference.

•••

Yvette brought the crystal flute of champagne to her lips as she shifted from one foot to the other. Her stilettos were gorgeous, absolute works of art, but they were little more than exquisite torture devices for her feet. After rushing between meetings and workshops all day, the pain was almost unbearable. Still, it would be a cold day in hell when she showed up at a conference in sensible shoes.

The elegant guests in the crowded hospitality suite laughed and chattered, as uniformed waiters served trays of elaborate appetizers and flutes of sparkling champagne. Industry events were absolutely necessary, but always such a bore. So little actually got accomplished until the conference was over and everyone was back at work, but the networking opportunities and connections one made were priceless. Yvette struggled to focus on the balding, paunchy man at her side droning on and on about how his company could help Saffron expand beyond chocolates, and why they were the perfect corporate match. She would give anything to meet someone interesting at one of these events for once, regardless of how they could help her career. Discreetly scanning the room, Yvette occasionally inserted what she hoped were appropriate sounds into the conversation and wished for a reprieve.

Her eyes settled on a vaguely familiar figure across the room. Richard Morgan swirled amber liquid in a cut crystal tumbler, looking as bored as she felt. The pictures she'd seen didn't do him justice. Images in print and online couldn't capture the sense of magnetism that surrounded him. That chiseled jawline, those striking green eyes, the way he seemed to command respect while completely at ease. She laid a gentle hand on her companion's forearm and flashed him a bright smile.

"Will you excuse me? I have somewhere I need to be." Without waiting for a reply, Yvette locked eyes with Richard and sashayed across the room as quickly as her delicate four-inch stiletto heels would allow. Now *this* could be interesting.

"Richard Morgan? Hi, I'm Yvette Cruz." She extended her hand to him and gave him her most professional smile. Good lord, he was handsome. She leaned in, close enough to smell his sophisticated fragrance, something lush and velvet, indefinable.

"I know who you are." His green eyes met hers in a steady gaze, and his expression gave nothing away. He didn't take her hand, and she let it drop to her side.

Yvette rearranged her features to hide her disappointment and paused for a beat, letting his icy reaction settle between them. She couldn't let him see that he had ruffled her. Shifting her weight to one leg, she pushed her shoulders back a bit, and dropped her chin so that she looked up at him through lowered lashes. "I'm so glad to finally meet you, though after spending so much time with your father, I feel like I know you already."

"I don't know what you mean, Ms. Cruz." His voice was low and deep, carefully controlled.

"Please, call me Yvette. No need for such formality." She laughed to break the tension and touched his arm. He flinched, almost imperceptibly, and kept his expression neutral. He was going to make her work for every word he uttered, but Yvette was never one to shy away from a challenge. Especially one this sexy.

He remained silent, so she continued. "I was hoping that we'd bump into one another here. I've been to the Morgan offices to meet with your father, but I could never quite catch up with you." His father never said yes to her proposals, but he was always glad to see her, was always welcoming and charming. Her encounters with Michael had been so pleasant that Richard's stonewall treatment blindsided her.

He took a sip of his drink and let out a short, humorless laugh. "Yes, I've seen you slinking around my father's office. You could have easily contacted my office to schedule a meeting with me, but I have a feeling that's not your style."

"What's that supposed to mean?"

"I just get the impression that you'd rather flirt with my father to get what you want than to deal with me directly. He's a sucker for a beautiful woman, but I am a bit more difficult to manipulate." He leveled her with a steely gaze. His eyes were intense, gorgeous, but filled with contempt.

"I have no idea what you're talking about. I've never flirted with your father, and that's not how I operate. Michael has always been charming and polite, but that's as far as it's ever gone. Our meetings have been strictly professional, unlike this conversation, and I resent the implication. It's not like I'm angling to become the fourth Mrs. Michael Morgan." She scoffed, a very unladylike sound, but his insinuation was unbelievable. Her instinct was to lash out, to defend her hard-won reputation and her professionalism, but Yvette took care to rein in her rising irritation, to keep her exterior controlled and cool. She wouldn't let him goad her into losing her temper. "I don't know why you'd expect me to schedule a meeting with you anyway. You've made it perfectly clear that you're not interested in the proposal. If my understanding is correct, your father is still the head of Morgan Confectioners." He took a small step back, apparently not prepared for her to call him out.

He paused for a beat before shaking his head, as though shaking off the remark. "He won't be in charge forever, Ms. Cruz, and unfortunately for you, he's taking my opinion on this matter under consideration. You're right, though. Meeting with me would be unnecessary as I have no interest in allowing Morgan Confectioners to be swallowed up by Saffron, and my answer will always be 'no' regardless of the offer. We're doing just fine on our own."

Yvette's lips formed a conciliatory smile. Morgan Confectioners was a sinking ship, and Saffron was itching to throw it a life vest. Richard was determined to deny that the other divisions were keeping it on life support, for whatever reason. She had to maintain control, show him that he couldn't rattle her with hostility. Time to kill him with kindness and professionalism, as she had a deal to broker. "Everyone would agree that Morgan Enterprises is doing fine, but your confections division is another story. You've got something we want, and I think we'd make a good team. What we're proposing would be good for everyone."

"You could dip that offer in your company's finest chocolate, and I still wouldn't bite."

He practically snarled, but she laughed. She had to admire his determination, as foolish as it seemed. "I assure you this is a sweet deal, even unembellished. We do pride ourselves on having the country's finest chocolate, though, and I'd be happy to send you some."

"Ms. Cruz," he said, adding emphasis on each syllable "I will never, under any circumstances, surrender on this issue."

"I can't decide if you sound more like a soap opera villain or a petulant child. Why can't we discuss this like adults, like professionals?"

"Because there's nothing to discuss."

"Have you even read our proposal? I'd be interested in hearing your thoughts, and I'd be happy to address any concerns you might have. At this stage, nothing is set in stone, and if there's something specific that you take issue with, I'd love to discuss it."

"No, I haven't read your proposal, and I'm not going to. I don't need to read it to know that I don't want Saffron's slick, generic mark on the products I love."

Now he went too far. Brand popularity didn't equal inferior product, and she wouldn't let Richard Morgan throw her off her game. "Saffron is known all over the country for our chocolate, and unlike Morgan, we're flourishing in a down economy." She flashed him a cool smile. "People love what we offer, and there's no reason to think we can't expect the same success with rebranded Morgan products."

"I'd rather be smaller but offer superior quality, rather than carelessly mass-producing and underpricing my competitors."

"And that's why your other divisions are outperforming confections by millions of dollars each year." She asserted sharply.

His eyebrow raised, and he sized her up with a narrowed gaze. Yvette shifted her weight, staring back and refusing to stand down as the tension strummed between them. "Touché, Ms. Cruz," he finally replied. Did the corner of his lips actually rise in a semblance of a smile or was that a trick of the low ballroom lighting?

"Listen, having wider distribution and a bigger marketing campaign doesn't mean you have to sacrifice quality. People in this country are still interested in originality and innovation. They just like buying from a brand they know, and they want it at a good price."

He frowned, considering. "You have a point, of course, but Morgan Confectioners is more to me than a revenue stream. It's a family business, something I care for very deeply."

She smiled. "I certainly understand the importance of family. I love mine, and owe everything I am to them. But didn't your father ever teach you that business and emotions don't mix?" Yvette took a chance and sidled closer, laying a hand on his arm and squeezing gently. "We love what you've developed so much that we want it for ourselves. You should be flattered," she added, her voice light and teasing. Any other man *would* be flattered. Why Richard Morgan was immune to her attention was a mystery.

He closed the distance between them and leaned down so that his lips almost touched her ear. His breath was hot against her skin and sent goose bumps erupting down her arms. He was close enough to kiss, and her breath caught in her throat as she waited to see what he would do.

"No. Deal." His firm words shouldn't have been arousing, but it was all she could do to resist the urge to find out what his mouth would feel like crushed against hers.

"Richard, this is the best offer you're likely to get. You should really give it some thought before you dismiss it." The sad truth was that if Saffron didn't buy them out, the confections division would continue to suck money from the rest of Morgan Enterprises until they found a way to turn it around.

"I've heard enough."

Yvette felt oddly disappointed by the finality of his words. Her lips wanted to find their way to his, to change his mind about *her*, if not the deal itself, but he turned and walked away.

Watching his broad back as he disappeared into the crowd, Yvette enjoyed the view despite herself. He would come around; they always did. Yvette Cruz didn't back down from a fight.

She'd come from nothing and had worked her whole life to get to where she was at Saffron Sweets. Everything she had, she had earned, and none of it had come easy what with her past. Nobody had given her a thing in life, ever, except for her parents, who had worked too hard for her to let a little setback like Richard Morgan stop her. Not after what she'd been through in her lifetime. Her hand fluttered subconsciously to her chest, her fingers tracing the ridged skin concealed by the high neckline of her dress.

To have her work belittled so casually, so flippantly, was infuriating. Almost as infuriating as her burning attraction to this man. She refused to accept that this would be their only encounter, and in truth, she couldn't wait to see what the next meeting would hold. After all, she always enjoyed a challenge.

Across the room, Richard approached a pretty brunette and stopped to chat. The other woman looked up at him with wide, adoring eyes, and as he smiled, laughed, and touched her arm, Yvette finally turned away. She finished her champagne with three long sips, set the empty glass on the nearest table, and strode toward the exit with her shoulders back and her head held high. As she passed Richard, she threw him a mental salute: *Till we meet again.*

• • •

Richard took a slow swallow of his single malt scotch, winced as it burned a trail down his throat, and watched Yvette glide out of the hospitality suite. What an aggravating temptation she was. Her cool, unflappable calm in the face of his disdain had just inflamed his desire more. Nobody stood up to him like that, ever, and part of him was eager to see what giving in to her would feel like—much to his dismay. The young food sciences chemist at his side was chattering excitedly about those effervescent lollipops she had developed for the company, and he knew he should give her his full attention, but his mind was on Yvette. Her obvious agenda irritated him, but her lush curves and impressively quick wit lingered in his mind, making it hard for him to remember why he'd wanted her gone. Beautiful women were easy to come by, but one with brains to match was a rare find, and one of his few weaknesses.

Richard was glad she'd left when she did though, as he'd been dangerously close to finding out if her lips were as soft and lush as they looked. He imagined they would be warm, and sweet with the champagne she'd been drinking. The thought gave rise to an unwelcome stirring deep within his body. What was wrong with him? The woman was after his company, and he had to remember that if he had any hope of protecting it. Focusing on the young brunette standing before him, he forced his mind off Yvette and her delicious curves. Or tried to.

" ...I mean, I was nervous at first, but the session went really well. I think everyone enjoyed it. I mean, they paid attention and asked a lot of questions when I finished." The young woman paused, apparently waiting for his response, and he snapped back to attention. She was filling him in on the discussion panel she had run that afternoon as a representative of their company, and she was obviously looking for praise.

He smiled down at her, turning on his signature charm. "I'm sure they did. Everybody wants something like your lollipops for their company. It's nice that you could provide some insight and maybe inspiration, but I'm certainly glad that Morgan Confectioners is the one that has you."

"You're so sweet to say so, Mr. Morgan. I'm glad to be a part of the company, and I hope to stay on after the buyout. I know that a lot of things change in these situations, but we're all praying that the department gets by relatively unscathed." She took a sip of her drink and watched him expectantly.

"Buyout? Rebecca," he watched her face to see if he got her name right, "there will be no buyout. Morgan has always been family owned, and we have no intention of changing that."

Her cheeks flushed, and her eyes darted around the room. "Oh, Mr. Morgan, I apologize. I suppose we've all heard the Saffron rumors and have obviously made more of it than was necessary. I shouldn't have said anything."

Richard relaxed his grip when he realized he was squeezing his glass almost hard enough to crack it. He hadn't expected news of his father's talks with Saffron to get out so quickly when so few people knew about them. Still, it was important for him to know what misinformation was circling, and he couldn't let his irritation show. "Saffron is looking to expand their product line beyond chocolate, and they've expressed interest in buying our confections division. But I've let them know in no uncertain terms that we're not interested. Anything you've heard is nothing more than conjecture. You've nothing to worry about."

Rebecca looked like she wanted to say more, but she sipped her champagne and remained silent. She shifted from one foot to the other, looking increasingly agitated, and Richard excused himself. He had obviously made her uncomfortable, and he was too distracted to make polite conversation with an employee. The scientist's relief was noticeable as he told her to enjoy the evening and wished her goodnight.

Richard finished his scotch in one burning swallow and set the empty tumbler on a table as he strode towards the door, anxious to get out of the room. He didn't know where he was headed, but it would be easier to think if he escaped the claustrophobic atmosphere of the crowded party. Yvette had invaded his business life and now had somehow managed to wind her way into his personal life, driving him to maddening distraction. She was beautiful—exquisite even—but he wasn't exactly inexperienced when it came to exceptional women. He never let personal matters interfere with his professional obligations. What was so different about her and how could he get her out of his system?

When she was just a name and face he'd glimpsed only briefly, he'd had a semblance of control. Now she was a three-dimensional threat to his sanity, and Richard needed to do something—anything—to push her off his radar. That would be nearly impossible when all he could think about was how soft her skin must be, how sweet her lips would taste beneath his.

He stormed out of the hospitality suite and punched the elevator button with much more force than necessary. Cursing both the wait and his uncharacteristic impatience, he pressed the button again.

"Will that make the elevator arrive faster?" The sultry voice matched the intoxicating fragrance invading his space and wound its way through his body.

So much for control.

Chapter Two

"Ms. Cruz. What a surprise." He tried to sound casual, unaffected, but her voice alone made his body respond, harden. Richard's unwelcome physical reaction to the sight of her, to her sweet but sensual fragrance, to the silky sound of her voice, frustrated him to no end. She was the enemy, but all he could think about was what the skin where her neck met her delicate ivory shoulders would taste like. Her brown eyes sparkled with amusement, and he hated that looking into them reminded him of melted pools of sweet, dark chocolate.

"It's nice to see you too. Going down?" She was bold, unruffled, even after he had stonewalled her.

The elevator doors opened, and they stepped in. The throaty laugh that escaped her glossy ruby lips pushed him over the edge.

"What's so funny, Ms. Cruz?"

"If you're so determined to shut me down, if you want so badly to be rid of me, then why not wait for the next elevator?"

"I'm not one to run from difficult situations. Or people." The fact that he wanted to kiss her as much as he wanted to tell her where she could shove her buyout offer was infuriating.

Her lips curled into a slow smile. "Now come on, I'm not that bad, am I?"

He jabbed at the floor button, ready to reach the lobby and escape. "No, but your company is certainly making my life miserable lately."

"That's the opposite of what—" The elevator stopped with a thud, hard enough to jostle them and throw Richard against Yvette.

Pinned against her, his body covering the yielding softness of hers, he couldn't think straight. His body responded instantly, broadcasting the thoughts he'd been trying too hard to suppress, and he found himself unable to look away when she gasped and met his gaze. He expected her to wriggle out of his arms, to clear her throat, anything to break the tension of the moment. Instead, she met his gaze, boldly, reflecting his own desire. Would she recoil or respond if he kissed her? With their faces inches apart, he could close the distance between them and satisfy his curiosity.

Her eyelids fluttered, and he inched closer until the elevator binged suddenly. Reluctantly he disengaged, moving back and putting space between them as the doors opened.

Richard took a cleansing breath, scraped a hand across his own jaw, and straightened his clothes. He stepped out of the elevator into the bustling lobby and without looking back, took Yvette by the arm and pulled her along beside him. They navigated their way through the crowd of tourists and employees, the bright lights and noise a jarring change from the hushed tension of the elevator. He could hear the clicking of her stiletto heels on the marble floor as she tried to keep up with him, but he steadfastly refused to meet her eye.

If he wanted the company of a beautiful woman, he should choose one of the many uncomplicated candidates he already knew. What was he doing dragging Yvette Cruz along when he should have left her in the elevator? He should turn his interest to someone more appropriate—someone who wasn't interested in taking the only thing he truly loved out of his control.

He took her hand, briefly noticed the buttery smoothness of her skin against his, and pulled her close. Tension strummed between them once more, and a hint of her spicy vanilla fragrance drifted towards him as he fought the urge to bury his face in her silky raven hair. "I don't know what happened in that elevator, but here's what's happening next. I'm going to buy you a drink, and then we're going to figure this out." He was back in control, dignified and assertive. Good. This was good.

"Nothing happened in there." She murmured, her voice like honey, though her expression said she was as rattled as he was.

He led Yvette to a busy casino bar and sucked in a breath as she perched on a brass barstool, crossing her legs and giving him an eyeful of creamy skin. She was like an exotic bird, each detail more exquisite than the last. Her dress clung to her curves, the slightly iridescent turquoise fabric standing out exotically in the sea of plain black clothes and frumpy tourists shuffling around them. Even her shoes were unique and beautiful, shaped to look like flowers. He imagined tossing those shoes on the floor and kissing his way from her toes up her legs, losing himself in the soft curves of her body. He shook his head slightly and cleared his throat.

"Mm. There's something so decadent about a beautiful flute of champagne. Don't you think?"

She appeared completely at ease, and he wondered if he was the only one who could feel the tension. If he didn't watch himself, he was liable to just give her the company. Richard had always been able to hold his liquor, but combined with her intoxicating effect, he was starting to worry about his judgment. Prying his eyes from Yvette, he ordered a club soda with lime and the cool bubbles helped clear his head and tame his libido. He had to focus on what was important here.

"So, tell me why my employees think that a deal with Saffron is all but inevitable."

She feigned innocence, her brows knitted together to form the tiniest crease in her forehead. "Pardon me?"

"Please don't insult me by pretending that you don't know what I'm talking about." He waved a hand up and down the length of her body. "I may have been momentarily distracted by the beautiful package, but now I want answers." He chewed on an ice cube, not sure if he'd gone too far.

She flinched, and anger flashed across her face, sharpening her features. "Beautiful package? What are you talking about?"

A short, rough laugh escaped him. "Seriously?" He paused and sighed. "Okay, we'll play it your way. I want to know how, when nothing more than a few private meetings have occurred, some of our employees know enough about your attempt to swipe Morgan Confectioners out from under me to be worried. Employees at the lab, at that, not even from the executive offices."

"I really have no idea what you're talking about, and I resent the implication that I'm somehow involved in subterfuge." She bit out the words, indignation flashing in her eyes.

"So you can look me in the eye and tell me that you have no hand in spreading this information?" His certainty faded as she sat beside him, her eyes sharp and devoid of deception.

She fixed him with a steady gaze, her almond-shaped deep brown eyes clear and unwavering. "Thank you for the drink, Mr. Morgan," She added sarcastic emphasis on his name. "I think it's time for me to say good night." Yvette slid off the barstool and took a moment to steady herself on her stilettos.

Whether she was an expert actress or really hadn't been spreading information about the buyout, he couldn't afford to let her leave just yet. His father consulted him as a courtesy, one that could be revoked as easily as it had been extended. Sending Yvette away in anger could provoke her to push even harder for the deal, and he needed all the time he could buy.

He put a hand on her arm. "Wait. Please."

She turned to face him, her expression challenging and exciting him despite himself. "Yes?"

He attempted a charming smile as he scrambled to find the right words. Knowing how it felt to have her slip from his grasp, he was determined to make amends. From what he could tell, she was far too savvy to be manipulated into setting aside her professional pursuits, but his mother had often said you'd catch more flies with honey than with vinegar. "I've offended you, and I'm very sorry, Yvette." Was it his imagination, or did her lips twitch into a smile at the sound of her name? "I was clearly wrong about you, and I want to apologize. I'm so passionate about the business that obviously my emotions can get heated, and I'm sorry you were caught up in that. Allow me to redeem myself and show you that I'm much more enjoyable to be around than I've led you to believe. Would you join me at the tables? Please?" He tilted his head towards the craps tables and kept his eyes locked on hers.

Her shoulders dropped and her expression softened a bit. "I suppose a couple of games won't hurt anything. You do owe me a pleasant evening, at least." She took the arm he offered, and he led her through the crowd towards the craps table.

Conversations swirled around them, and the barrage of sights and sounds assaulted them. The simulated daylight inside the hotel made the charged energy between them seem surreal, almost like a dream. The thoughts going through his mind were definitely of the midnight variety. They found a table with room for them to join the game, and he guided Yvette to his side. It was time to regain control of himself and the situation.

•••

The craps table was crowded with jubilant gamblers cheering and watching the dice bounce across the table. Yvette felt the charged energy of the crowd but was too rattled to pay much attention to the games.

He appeared willing enough to make amends, seemed to feel the same magnetic pull towards her that she felt for him, in fact. Against her better judgment, she wanted to let him win her over, to make up for what he'd said, to change her mind about him. She decided that she'd allow herself to relax as long as he continued to behave himself.

He raised an eyebrow, a roguish, tempting expression on his face. "What do you say? Want to play?" Why did she get the impression that he wasn't only referring to the craps game?

"Sure, though I should warn you that I've never played before. Craps looks like so much fun, but it's intimidating when you have no idea what's going on."

He snaked his hand around her waist and squeezed. "I'll be gentle." His arm around her was warm and inviting, and her misgivings faded a bit. They took their places at the table and he exchanged cash for a stack of casino chips. He gave her a handful and said, "Okay, just put the green chip over there on the pass line and we'll be in the game." He indicated a place on the table and she placed their bet. "The shooter is in the middle of a roll. He's going to roll the dice and try to get the point number, which is nine. Don't worry about trying to figure it out. You'll pick it up as we go along."

Despite herself, Yvette found that she enjoyed his gentle direction and friendly charm. There was no hint of the hostility that laced their earlier conversations. She wanted to hold back, to exercise a little caution before giving in to his advances, but it was hard. With considerable effort, she forced herself to focus on his words and not the sensual shape of his lips. The lips she would've tasted had the elevator not stopped.

The shooter rolled the dice and the crowd around the table watched them fly from one end of the table to the other before emitting a collective groan as the dice showed seven. She looked up at Richard. "Why is everybody disappointed?"

"He crapped out. He rolled a seven before rolling a nine, so basically, his turn is over and we're up. Do you want to play?"

She shook her head. "Why don't you play for both of us? I'll just watch for now. If it's possible, I'm even more confused than before."

He took two dice from the handful offered by the stickman and held them to her lips. "Kiss them for luck." She touched her lips to the dice in his hand and watched as he tossed them across the table. She didn't know what numbers she was hoping for, but she held her breath as she waited to see what would come up. They bounced to a stop at the far end of the table and she saw a five and a six. The crowd went wild, jumping and cheering.

"Eleven. Everyone's excited because it's an automatic payout for them. They all make money when I roll a seven or eleven. Another kiss?" What she wanted was kiss from him, but she touched her lips to the dice and watched him fling them across the felt again. His throw yielded another eleven, and the crowd went wild cheering as they threw down more bets. She still didn't completely understand it, but the enthusiasm was infectious. "That's another payout for the crowd. I'm on a roll—you must be my lucky charm, Yvette." He favored her with a sexy smile and a smoldering look.

Richard held the dice to her lips again and she gave them another kiss. He threw the dice across the table and the crowd watched until eight was revealed, a four and a four. Looking down at her, he slid an arm around her waist. "So eight is my point number. Now everyone will back up their bets and place extra bets in hopes of me hitting my point or any other number before rolling a seven."

He held the dice out expectantly and she kissed them again, shaking her head at how such a successful and competent businessman could be superstitious. The dice bounced against the far edge with his toss and settled on a four and a six.

Richard flipped a black $100 chip onto the table and addressed the dealers. "The hard way. This one's for the boys." She gave him a curious look, and he explained. "It's a tip for the dealers. They'll know what to do with it. You really are bringing me luck tonight. What do you say we raise the stakes?" His breath was warm on her neck, his voice low and enticing. A delicious shiver skipped down her spine at his words.

"What do you have in mind?" She realized that her voice was breathy and ridiculous, but Richard had a potent effect on her.

One so powerful she grew tired of resisting and wondered what would happen if she simply gave in to her attraction. What would it hurt, really?

He shot her a rakish grin and a thrill trembled through her, shooting straight through to her core. "If I roll an eight on my next turn, you spend the night with me."

● ● ●

"Spend the night together? Wow, you don't waste any time."

She arched an eyebrow, but her cool reply was undermined by the sparkling amusement in her eyes. It'd been a gamble, but he never got anything he wanted in life by holding back. Removed from the buyout discussion, Yvette was exactly the kind of woman he wanted, beautiful and smart, savvy and ambitious. He'd never be able to stop thinking about their near kiss in the elevator, and unless he was wrong, she hadn't stopped either.

"And if you don't roll an eight?"

"That's your choice." He waited for her response, his eyes focused and intense. "Tomorrow morning, I'll be on a plane heading back home. I don't waste time, because I don't have any to spare. You don't have to do anything you don't want to do, of course."

Richard held his breath as she tilted her head, considering. "All right." It took all his willpower to let her finish her sentence instead of scooping her up and carrying her back to the suite. "If you don't roll an eight, you'll buy me dinner."

He gave her an incredulous look. "That's it? I throw out spending the night together, and all you ask for is a dinner? Seems like I may have overshot."

"Yes, that's it. After dinner, who knows where the night will lead?" He swallowed hard at the sultry tone of her voice. "First, though, I want you to agree to sit down to a meal with me, during which you will listen to me and carefully consider my proposition."

"I almost expected you to ask me to consent to the acquisition outright. I'm surprised you didn't throw the buyout in for the bet."

She frowned. "Despite what you think of me, I don't want you to hand me your company. Like I told you, I don't enjoy taking what I didn't earn.

"Fair enough. It appears that I may have underestimated you. So do we have a deal?"

Even considering taking Yvette to bed was reckless. He knew it, and yet had no desire to pull back on the agreement. He wanted her, whether it was a good idea or not. She'd managed to blur the lines between business and pleasure, and his determination to keep his distance from her felt very far away. If the dice fell in his favor, he'd worry about redefining their boundaries later.

"It's a deal."

He pulled her close, tucking an errant strand of hair behind her ear, and let his hand linger at her jaw, before turning his attention back to the game. Yvette kissed the dice that he proffered, and he tossed them across the table. This was it. Richard held his breath as he watched the dice bounce, head buzzing as the noisy crowd faded into the background. His stomach flipped when one four and then another came up. Another eight.

The hard way.

Chapter Three

Yvette let him take her hand as they wound through the crowded casino towards the elevator, concentrating all her energy on not shaking in her stilettos. This was crazy, wasn't it? She didn't just glide up to a suite with a man she barely knew because he rolled some dice. It was crazy, but damned if she wasn't going to do it.

The moment the elevator doors closed, Richard pulled her closer and pressed a kiss to her lips. She opened her mouth to his, and their tongues tangled together as they explored and tasted each other. His mouth was cool, with only the faintest hint of the lime from his club soda, but warmed as their kiss deepened. Desire swirled within her, clouding her with an intoxicating sweetness that made her misgivings seem far away.

Spending a passionate night in bed with her corporate target might not be the savviest business move, but she would never overcome this insane attraction to him if she walked away. She'd obsess about him, wondering what might have been, imagining what she had missed. Perhaps giving in just this once would sate her desire and she'd be able to think clearly again. Then she could walk away without regret, couldn't she? It didn't have to affect the acquisition. Nothing had to change between them. She'd do her job, and he'd do his. Their night together would be little more than a memory once they returned to Philly.

Of course, they would have the memories, and she'd have to work even harder on the Morgan buyout to convince him that she hadn't used sex to get what she wanted.

"What is it?" Richard must have seen the indecision on her face as she pulled away.

She took a deep breath and exhaled, considering how much to reveal. "This is moving really quickly, especially since just hours ago you actively disliked me. I have to ask myself if this is a good idea." She chewed on her bottom lip, feeling exposed after her admission. It felt strange to admit misgivings after the passionate kiss they'd shared, but she had never been able to completely separate sex from emotion. She didn't need him to be in love with her, but she wouldn't be able to respect herself if she slept with someone who didn't even like her.

He ran his fingers over her cheek, gazing down into her eyes. "When we met, I didn't dislike you, I was only trying to distance myself to protect my company. I had no way of knowing that I'd be unable to keep my hands off of you. As it turns out, I actually like you very much." He grinned. "You're the first woman I've met in a long time who isn't afraid to call me out when I sound like a soap opera villain. How could I resist?"

God, but he was sexy. A flush of attraction warmed her body, straight to her toes, and she took his hand, rubbing her thumb across his knuckles. "Well, when you put it that way…" The elevator slowed to a stop on the floor for conference attendees. "I'll get my things and meet you in your room."

"The Charlemagne Suite." His gaze was hungry and intense. "Don't keep me waiting."

The doors opened, and she stepped into the hallway on unsteady legs. His eyes never left hers as the doors closed behind her, promising a night she wouldn't soon forget. She fumbled in her tiny beaded clutch for her key as she walked down the hallway. Stepping into the cool silence of her hotel room, Yvette closed the door behind her. If she was going to clear her head and make a rational decision, now would be the time. She flipped on the light, waiting for the realization that she was about to make a big mistake to hit her. Nothing.

She gathered her clothes and the personal items she would need and considered whether or not it would be smarter to stay put. Of course it would be smarter, who was she kidding? She could call the whole thing off right now, and probably should. As dangerous as spending a night in the arms of Richard Morgan would be, the thought of not going through with it was almost painful. Surely they could forget about business for one night, and simply be a man and a woman. Nothing more.

She rarely went to bed with a man she wasn't in love with, much less one she wasn't sure she even liked. The candy industry was a small one and Richard one of the larger players in it. He was a very public figure, and Yvette had read countless articles about him. She knew that he was thirty-two, that he had an Ivy League education, and that his mother had been in a fatal automobile accident around twenty years ago. His younger brother had been in the accident too, but had survived and now ran a successful record label in New York.

His former wife, on the other hand, had been photographed so often that though the couple had been divorced for years, Yvette could still picture Chelsea Morgan clearly. Their divorce had been acrimonious and very public, their disdain for each other ongoing, recorded in detail in the local media's gossip reports. Was that why Richard had been so quick to assume Yvette was some sort of gold digging sexpot?

The company's profits were legendary, but Michael Morgan's inheritance insured that the family fortune would be virtually limitless regardless of which direction the business took. Richard was a brilliant businessman, and he was heavily involved with philanthropy as well, whether out of genuine charity or to improve his public image, she didn't know. He personally donated a sizable percentage of his income and personal time every year to a pediatric cancer charity. Thoughtful, she lifted her hand to her chest and absently ran her fingertips across the scar there again.

Having now met the man, she could see that while Richard Morgan was practically perfect on paper, there was a wall around him. A cynicism that would usually keep her from trying to get close, but there was something interesting, fascinating even, about him. Yvette had a feeling that spending a night with him would be an adventure she wouldn't regret.

With a final check in the mirror, she zipped her overnight bag closed and pulled the strap over her shoulder. As her hotel room door closed quietly behind her, her hesitation fell away and she strode towards the elevator, looking forward to the night ahead.

•••

Her position at Saffron had her spending nearly as much time in hotels as she did at home, but she'd never stayed in a suite so opulent and luxurious. The house she grew up in, mere blocks from one of the busiest drug and prostitution corners in the state, made this place look like a palace. She looked up to Richard with wide eyes, and he laughed indulgently. "It's a bit much, isn't it? Dad and I hosted a cocktail reception here for the reps from a beverage company we're working with, so I could justify the expense."

Yvette feared her sophisticated veneer was slipping. "It's certainly a bit grander than Saffron's corporate budget allows." Hell, it was the fanciest digs she'd ever seen in her lifetime.

Normally, she didn't like to reveal any weaknesses to her business rivals, but what the heck. They were about to get much more intimate than two competitors had any business being. Why not drop the façade for a night?

"Come on in. Make yourself at home." He led her through the sitting room, past a well-stocked bar, an actual full-sized dining room, and into the bedroom. The sumptuous royal blue linens on the king-sized bed seemed to both beckon and mock her with their inviting textures and softness.

An ornate golden stand held an ice bucket with a bottle of champagne, two delicate cut crystal champagne flutes, and a bowl of beautiful ripe strawberries. She thought it was a bit cliché, but had to admit that the effect was decadent and romantic. A bittersweet longing tugged her heart, and she sank down into the plush, velvety loveseat situated in the bedroom.

"This suite is simply unbelievable, Richard. Everything is so exquisite." She waved her hand around the room, finding no words adequate enough to describe their opulent surroundings.

"*You* are exquisite, Yvette." Would he think so when he saw her jagged scar and chemical burns? He plucked a champagne flute off the table and handed it to her before expertly popping the cork of the chilled bottle of Taittinger. He filled her glass and handed it to her before filling his own, his fingertips lightly brushing hers. The brief contact set her heart racing, pounding hard. "To a beautiful woman, and a beautiful night together," he said as he raised his glass in toast. He took a sip of his champagne as she did the same, and he stepped closer to join her on the loveseat but stopped short. Her posture was ramrod straight, but a bouncing knee betrayed her nerves. "You seem nervous. Is everything okay?" He took another sip from his glass and watched her with concern in his eyes. Candlelight danced in the shadows of the room, making Richard even more irresistibly sexy than before.

She squirmed and took a sip of champagne, watching the bubbles race to the top as she considered how to best answer the question. Should she pretend that she was the kind of woman for whom one night of no-strings-attached sex was commonplace? Telling him that she wasn't the kind of woman who usually did what she was about to do would just sound silly. This wasn't the time to look for validation or try to extract meaning from the situation. This was the time to release her inhibitions and give in to the desire brewing between the two of them. Only then would it be out of her system so she could move on. She gave Richard her best smile. "Everything's fine."

Yvette was rewarded with a wolfish grin and a rakish look in his eyes. "Come here." His deep baritone sent a shiver through her and she met his gaze with her own. Rising and walking to where he stood, she fleetingly wished that the room was dimmer, but was too excited about the prospect of seeing and tasting more of him to give it much more thought. She didn't relish the idea of him seeing her less than perfect body, her scar, or the light chemical burns that dusted her fair skin, but with any luck he would be enough of a gentleman to overlook her flaws. She was practiced at presenting a certain image, highlighting her best features and hiding the rest. But Richard Morgan didn't seem to be the kind of man who did things halfway, least of all in the bedroom.

He didn't notice her hesitation. "I want you now, all of you, and waiting is taking all of my willpower." He took her champagne flute and placed it by his on the table. "Now turn around." She turned her back to him and he unzipped her dress, letting it fall to the floor. He turned her around to face him and held her hands as she stepped out of the dress, leaving it behind in a heap. His masterful control of the situation gave her no choice but to comply.

She kept her gaze cast down, unable to look him in the eye. He broke the silence, his voice raspy, thick with desire. "Gorgeous. Absolute perfection. Look at me, Yvette." His fingertips traced the scar on her collarbone, and his eyes widened in surprise. He tipped her chin up with a fingertip until she raised her face and met his gaze. When she looked in his eyes, he held her gaze, didn't scan her body, didn't recoil when he noticed the chemical burns she'd been so worried would disgust him. In his eyes she saw sincerity… and lust. He wasn't lying; she really was beautiful in his eyes. He reached up and plucked pins from her hair, tossing them carelessly to the floor until raven waves fell freely around her shoulders. Weaving his fingers into her hair, he gripped gently, pulling her closer until their lips met, close enough for a kiss. His breath danced across her lips as he whispered, "I've wanted to run my fingers through your hair since the first moment I saw you.

It was definitely worth the wait." He crushed his lips against hers and kissed her with surprising intensity until she felt her body respond to his.

Her body was thrumming with excitement, and her mind clouded with the intensity of the feelings that Richard had awakened within her. His hands explored her curves as though every inch of her body fascinated him, and she luxuriated in the contrast of his warm skin against her cool softness. She slid his jacket off his shoulders and tossed it aside, loosened his tie until she could pull it off, threw it behind him, and began unbuttoning his shirt as he trailed, hot, insistent kisses down her neck. Pushing his shirt over his shoulders, Yvette kicked it aside when it fell to the floor. As she stepped back, an appreciative noise escaped her lips.

She ran her hands over the hard planes of muscle covering his stomach, then around his waist to his back as he pulled her into his arms. Pressing herself against him to accept another deep kiss, she faintly registered a ping of surprise as he deftly unfastened the clasp of her bra. Once she moved again, once she was no longer pressed against him, it would fall to the ground and she would be on display to him, imperfections and all. She didn't want to stand before him naked and exposed while he was still half-dressed. Her hands found his belt and worked quickly to unfasten the buckle, unbutton his pants and pull down the zipper. She pushed his pants down with enough force for them to reach the floor, and he stepped out of them, lifting her and wrapping her legs behind his back in one swift motion. In his arms, she felt light, feminine, and irresistible. Their lips never left one another's as he carried her to the bed and laid her down beneath him.

Yvette lost herself in the magic of his kiss and released her inhibitions when he pulled her bra over her arms and tossed it onto the floor. He rocked back onto his knees and surveyed her bare torso with naked appreciation in his eyes. Candlelight flickered all around them, and his eyes were a pool of hazy lust as he gazed upon her body. Under his spell, she forgot to be self-conscious about her scar, her imperfections, the light marks that marred her skin. He ran a fingertip across her scar and leaned down to plant light, teasing kisses down her neck, over to her shoulder, and finally to the base of her neck. As her body responded to his, she was certain that she would explode with lust before he was even completely undressed.

He moved his mouth to her breast and licked long, languorous strokes from the bottom to the top, over and over until she could take no more. She took his head in her hands and planted him firmly in the center of her breast, where he obliged by pulling her into his mouth with gentle but insistent force. A soft moan escaped her lips, and he responded by moving to the other breast. His hands never stopped moving, their expert strokes driving her mad with passion. She ran her fingers through his hair, luxuriating in the soft feel of the dark locks in her hands. Richard turned his attention further down her body, running his tongue over the planes of her stomach, both thrilling her and unnerving her. There were few parts of her body that Richard hadn't seen and showered with attention. The tiny turquoise lace panties she wore were all that separated her from him, and he was circling them with whispery, hot kisses, and her breath caught when he pulled them down over her legs. They fluttered to the floor after being carelessly tossed aside, and he gently pushed her thighs apart. He took a moment to indulge in a long, appreciative look and a sexy smile spread across his lips. She heard a low moan deep in his throat as he lowered his head and touched his lips to the apex of her thighs. He planted kisses all around her most sensitive area, his breath hot on her body. Just when she thought she would lose control, his tongue ran long, lazy strokes against her center before swirling circles around her most sensitive point. His fingers and mouth worked in tandem to drive her into a frenzy of pleasure. Mindlessly, she cried out Richard's name as passion clouded her mind and she felt as though she had come undone beneath his mouth and hands. Intense waves of exquisite sensation rolled over her, and she opened up to him completely and without hesitation. She lost all sense of modesty as he took her over the edge of passion with his touch. Never before had she dreamed that a man's touch could bring her such intense pleasure.

He raised himself up on his arms once more, hovering over her body close enough that she could feel his breath on her skin. A delicious shiver skipped down her spine as he moved up her body, dotting her skin with kisses as he moved, licking and nipping her along the way. He stretched out beside her and pulled her into his embrace. She ran her fingers up and down the length of his body, from his hip to his shoulder, as he kissed the top of her head and loosened his grip on her enough to lie back and relax. His fingertips traced a lazy circle on her shoulder.

"Thank you." As soon as the words were out of her mouth, she laughed at their absurdity.

She heard a low, quiet laugh in Richard's throat as he inhaled against her hair and kissed her sweetly on the top of her head. "It was my pleasure."

"That was amazing. I really needed that after the stress I've been under the last couple of weeks."

"Plotting to take over innocent candy companies can really take it out of you, huh? Glad I could help." With soft laughter, he traced the curves from her shoulder down to her hip and whispered against her skin.

He hardened against her, sending warmth blooming from deep within her, making her ache for him, desperate for him to fill her. Her body arched to meet his as she returned his kisses with growing intensity while soft moans escaped her throat. Before she knew it, his undergarments were on the floor and he sheathed himself in a condom. Positioning himself between her legs, eyelids heavy with desire, he buried himself within her.

· · ·

As they lay together in the dim light, her limbs were rubbery with delicious fatigue. Her eyes drifted closed, and his finger traced over her scar, nudging her from her drowsiness.

"Is this a MediPort scar?"

"Yes, I had cancer when I was a teenager. These are the chemical burns from the radiation treatment." She pointed out the light marks on her skin. His lavish attention made it easy to forget that she had been self-conscious about the scars and imperfections earlier. The extensive work he did for local pediatric cancer charities meant that he'd likely seen much worse than her scar. So much of her body image was wrapped up in the imperfections that it was hard to believe that they weren't glaring to someone who'd seen it all before.

"Oh my God, Yvette, I had no idea. What kind of cancer? Are you in remission?" The concern in his voice touched her and made her want to open up to him. He was making it so difficult to remember that their affair would last only until dawn.

"I was diagnosed with stage two Hodgkin's disease when I was seventeen. I had chemotherapy and radiation treatments for about a year, and at this point I'm considered cured. I had to go in for regular checkups for a few years before my doctors felt confident that I was completely clear, but I've been cancer free for quite awhile now."

"I'm so glad for that." He kissed her lips softly. "I know a few kids with that diagnosis, and the chemo and radiation is never easy, regardless of the prognosis. What a horrible thing to go through."

"It was a pretty miserable year, and if I had my choice I certainly wouldn't choose to go through it again, but the cancer really is part of who I am. It brought me closer to my family, and it gave me a great deal of perspective at an early age." Her cancer diagnosis and subsequent treatment were far enough in her past that she had made her peace with the experience. "It's made me appreciate the things I have and what I can accomplish, in a way that having a normal childhood might not have."

"I've heard similar things from other cancer survivors. Sounds like you turned a terrible situation into a positive." He pulled her close again and kissed her gently as she snuggled against him, marveling at the perfect fit.

"It hasn't always been easy. The treatment changed my life forever, and not always in a good way. Nobody ever complained or resented me, but I know it was so hard for the whole family. The treatment took forever and was incredibly expensive, even with insurance, and my parents were strapped financially. My poor sister was the one always stuck sitting with me during chemo, and I wasn't exactly easy to get along with. She was so good about trying to entertain me while we sat in the treatment room for hours, but I didn't exactly appreciate her sacrifice. She was fifteen and would've definitely rather have been at the mall with her friends."

"I'm sure she was happy to be with you. I have a younger brother, and we never went through anything like that, but I would do the same for him. She was probably scared out of her mind that they'd lose you."

"After a while, it became our family's normal. My doctors were great about managing my treatment schedule so I had my worst days on weekends and I hardly ever missed school. If it hadn't been for my bad days and the constant insomnia, we probably could've pretended that everything was fine."

"So, business as usual at the Cruz house?"

"Yeah, after a while I gave up on playing the cancer card." She laughed, remembering. "At first, I got out of a lot of housework and chores, even got away with treating the family badly, but it wasn't long before they started calling me out on my behavior again. Especially my sister."

"Siblings will do that." His chest rumbled under her cheek.

Yvette shifted next to him. "She was the one who finally told me that cancer was no excuse for being a jerk. As soon as she said it, I could tell that she wished she could take it back. Our parents were always on her case to help me out, to watch over me, to take care of me. She was so shocked that it came out of her mouth that we just cracked up. It was such a relief to be with her after that, to have at least one person see me for who I was and not something that could break at the slightest touch."

"I have a hard time thinking of you as fragile."

"Having cancer can teach you a lot. A lot of people feel like they have a new lease on life, or think life is precious and it needs to be appreciated. Well, it taught me that there's no excuse big enough to stop me."

His laughter rumbled. "I can definitely see that."

"It was good to be reminded that I was more than a cancer patient. My sister was right to call me out on my behavior." Everyone else had been too afraid to upset her, would've let her do whatever she wanted as long as they could ignore what was happening to her. "I knew she was worried for me, though. She'd sit up with me a lot of the time when I couldn't sleep, watching bad television and getting me candy since that's the only thing I could tolerate. That's probably when I started my love affair with confections."

"Candy has certainly treated you well."

"Oh yeah. I wish everything that came from the cancer was as satisfying."

"You still have lingering effects?"

"Not symptoms or anything, no. I don't worry about the cancer returning, not after being in remission so long at least, but the doctor said the radiation effectively destroyed my chances of ever having children. I've made my peace with that, more or less, but it's been a lot to take."

Made her peace was a deliberate overstatement. Yvette understood that she wouldn't be a mother—not biologically at least—but she'd never been okay with it. Nurturing her career like the child she'd never have had filled the void in a way, but the desire to have a family, a real family, had never been satisfied.

So few people in her adult life knew about the cancer, and fewer still knew about her infertility. Her relationships were generally superficial, never drifting into deeper territory than when and where they'd meet for drinks or dinner. Talking about it with Richard was strangely soothing, as though she could share without judgment.

"I think that's something I've always taken for granted, probably because I've never given a lot of thought to whether or not I want to be a father." Richard tilted his head to the side, his reaction more thoughtful than she would've anticipated.

"If I never had the treatment, I probably wouldn't have given it much thought either. Growing up, especially in a family like mine, I just assumed I'd be a mother some day. I don't know if I would've changed my mind as I got older, but I would've liked to have had the choice, you know?"

They drifted into silence, lost in thought, as she wondered at the wisdom of divulging so much intensely personal information. Especially to a man she hardly knew. Still, it didn't feel that way any longer. Richard's breath was hot against her skin, and for the briefest moment, she thought about what a life with him would be like. She gave herself a mental shake. This was one night, and one night only. In fact, it might be far wiser to end this before reality settled in. Was she going to spend the whole night in bed beside him? Surely retreating to her hotel room would be far wiser, and for all she knew he was waiting politely for her to make her exit. Though her body protested at every movement, she pulled herself up, carefully extricating herself from his embrace. As she swung her legs over the side of the bed, he caught her and playfully pinned her beneath him.

"Going somewhere?" His lips were hot on her neck, over her collarbone, leaving goose bumps in their path. His hands held her wrists, gently but firmly, and suddenly the idea of leaving this bed seemed very far away.

"Did you have something else in mind?" Her lips twisted into a saucy grin as she rolled back towards him in bed, ready to move away from the serious direction their conversation had taken and more than willing to see what else he had to offer.

Chapter Four

Richard awoke the next morning to find the pillow next to his empty, then stretched and turned over onto his back as he heard the faint sound of the shower. Yvette was still here. A satisfied smile spread across his face as he thought of her lush body lying beneath him last night, the sweet taste of her, how her kisses burned a trail on his skin. That smooth, soft neck. The gentle, desperate sound of her voice in the darkness, as they'd indulged their desire for one another throughout the night. He felt his body respond, harden, as he imagined her standing in the shower, steam floating around her, water cascading over her curves, her slim waist giving way to soft rounded hips. He eased himself out of bed and padded across the suite to the bathroom.

Richard hesitated outside the closed bathroom door and considered himself in the mirror. He had to laugh as he pictured her reaction to seeing him appear in her shower, naked and disheveled from sleep. His hair stuck out all about his head, a light stubble covered his face, and pillow marks were still visible across his forehead. His appearance wouldn't stop him, though. Their agreement had only been for one night, and while he had certainly made good use of his time, he had to go to her again before she left. Richard's desire for Yvette had been awoken with a vengeance, and he couldn't wait to sate it. Quietly opening the door, he peeked inside the steam-filled bathroom and quickly crossed the room to join her in the shower.

...

Richard wandered into the dining room of the suite, dressed in lounge pants and a T-shirt, unable to wipe the satisfied smile from his face. Yvette was sitting at the suite's desk, poring over the room service menu. She was professionally dressed; her overnight bag was packed and zipped closed, waiting in the sitting area. Clearly, she was ready to move on. Was he the only one who wanted to prolong their time together? Surely after the night they'd spent together, having breakfast wouldn't be a stretch.

"What looks good?"

"Hmm. I was just thinking coffee." She yawned. "Could use a little pick me up before the long flight home."

He had to laugh at that. "I guess we didn't get much sleep last night. You won't sleep on the plane?"

"I've never been able to relax enough. Even on international flights, I have a hard time getting quality rest and usually don't sleep until I pass out from exhaustion."

"Let's get you some caffeine, then." He picked up the menu and scanned the choices. "And a little breakfast? You've got to eat."

She agreed, and he called down to have food sent up. Had it been anyone else, it would've been awkward to sit in the suite, waiting for room service, after the night—and morning—they'd experienced. He wanted breakfast with her, and then some. Getting even a small glimpse into who Yvette was and forgetting for a night that she was his biggest corporate threat made him want to prolong their time together. If he had to marry in order to gain control over the confections division, he'd want it to be to someone like her. Or that there was a way that it could be her. An engagement to Yvette would effectively eliminate the trouble of their divergent professional goals, leaving him with everything that he wanted. It was intriguing, but ridiculous. She'd never agree to it.

The room service attendant arrived and set their order on the dining room table while Richard signed for the expenses. Yvette poured coffee for both of them, and he sneaked a glance at the domestic scene while he ushered the attendant out. Once he started thinking of them having a future, it was easy to picture her at home, pouring coffee, eating breakfast, living a normal life. As the door closed behind him, he swept the foolish daydream from his mind and joined her at the table. She pushed a cup of coffee towards him, and he sipped, sighing gratefully as the caffeine entered his system.

"Perfect, thank you." He filled a plate with eggs and fruit while she did the same. They ate in companionable silence for a bit, until Yvette pushed her plate away and rose. "Leaving already?"

"I've got a few things to wrap up before I catch my flight. I'll see you around?" Without waiting for an answer, she hoisted her bag's strap over her shoulder and headed for the door.

"Wait!" His voice stopped her in her tracks.

She hesitated, one hand on the door, and turned back to face him. "Yes?"

"Just because our agreement was for one night doesn't mean you have to run out of here at the first opportunity." He held out a hand, beckoning her.

"I'm not running out," she said, though she looked back towards the door as she said it, before slowly making her way back towards him. "It's just time for me to go."

"Maybe you could stay for a few more minutes? Once you leave, it's over." Richard's voice dropped as she reached him, and he smoothed a loose strand of hair behind her ear. "I'm not sure I'm ready for it to be over. I don't know why I thought I'd be able to forget you if we spent the night together. What was I thinking?"

Worry lines creased her forehead. "Do you regret it?"

He laughed, a deep rumbling in his chest. "I don't regret a single moment of our time together. I just expected to feel ready to move on, and instead I want you more."

He was surprised at his own confession, but amazingly he didn't regret telling her how he truly felt. Richard pulled her into his arms and leaned in, their lips meeting in a kiss seared with longing. But too soon, Yvette pulled away.

"I've got to go. Goodbye, Richard." Without meeting his eyes, she picked up her bag and let herself out of his suite.

•••

Yvette sipped her spicy bloody Mary and settled back in her seat, ready for her flight home to Philadelphia and glad that Saffron had sent her first class. She was exhausted, hungry, and emotional. A seat in coach wouldn't cut it today. She popped a few warm almonds in her mouth and snuggled underneath her plush throw blanket while she contemplated watching a movie or reading a book instead of catching up on work.

None of the options sounded appealing however. She was too consumed by the memories of their final kiss. The way he'd enveloped her in his embrace, surrounding her with his warmth and the clean scent of the soap he'd just used. It had overcome her, the emotions too much, and she'd practically dashed out of his room. He probably thought she was nuts.

The cocktail was slowly loosening her limbs, but suddenly a faint tension strummed within her and the energy in the cabin shifted. Afraid she already knew what she would find, she leaned around the seat beside hers and found her face inches away from Richard's hip as he stuffed items in the overhead bin.

She hated how her body responded so easily at the mere sight of him. Proximity to this man shouldn't turn her into a puddle, but when he looked down at her, his lips curled into a sexy smile and she warmed from head to toe. She shifted back until she was upright in her own seat and composed herself.

"Hi, Richard," she said in greeting, her tone chagrined and bemused. Of course they'd have the same flight back. She was pleased that even though her insides wobbled at the sight of him, her voice was clear and steady.

"Hi, Yvette," he said with a nod, an amused look on his gorgeous face, too. Just hearing her name on his lips sent a frisson of electricity straight to her core. He had to see how he affected her. He took his seat next to hers and settled in. "So, this is cozy, you and me, together on the long flight home."

"Who knew you flew commercial? I would think Richard Morgan only traveled by private jet." She teased, hoping to dispel the tension that was threatening to strangle her.

He accepted his snack and a drink from the flight attendant and laughed indulgently. It was a deep, throaty laugh, low enough that it was just for her. "My jet is in the shop, and besides, I had airline miles that were about to expire."

"How very practical of you," she deadpanned. What was he doing here? What were the chances that they were randomly assigned adjoining seats? That couldn't have just happened.

"You disappeared this morning. Now we'll have a chance to get to know each other." His tone was light as he relaxed into his seat next to her. How was this so easy for him? Yvette didn't know if she wanted to run away or straddle him in his seat.

The wild passion they shared seemed like an erotic dream in the cold light of day, and their morning encounter in the shower might as well have happened in another lifetime.

"Forgive me if I'm a bit confused, but I thought you wanted one night together with no strings attached. I don't see how that includes sharing intimate conversations on this flight home."

He sipped his drink and paused before responding. He looked down at his glass and shook it gently, the ice cubes clinking against the sides. "To be perfectly honest, I know that I should have changed my flight. When we get back to Philly, it's in my best interest, and probably yours as well, to go our separate ways and pretend that last night never happened. I can't see much harm in sharing a pleasant flight together, though. I really enjoyed our time together." He raked his gaze up and down her body before meeting her eyes. "If I'm not mistaken, you did too."

She struggled to remain calm and composed as she cast her gaze down at her lap. "Well, yes, I did too."

Saying that she enjoyed their time together was an understatement. Sitting so close to him on the plane brought images of his hard, bronze body underneath the expensive-looking custom-tailored suit he wore. She caught the occasional whiff of his lush, warm scent when he shifted in his seat and fought the urge to bury her nose against his skin and inhale deeply. He loosened his silvery green tie and unbuttoned his top button before draining his drink. Her eyes were drawn to the hands that had touched every part of her just hours ago. Remembering how his expert hands felt sliding across her wet, soapy skin brought a hot flush to her cheeks.

She reluctantly turned her attention to the flight attendant's safety instructions as the crew readied for takeoff. Richard was close enough to touch, but he maintained just enough distance to keep her guessing. Surreptitiously, Yvette studied his profile. This could be trouble.

Within no time, the plane was in the air, and they gave their lunch orders to the flight attendant. Then she angled her body to face him. "Can I ask you something? If you're absolutely determined to refuse my company's offer, then what's the harm in being seen together?"

"It wouldn't look good for me to be seen with you. I probably shouldn't have even been with you last night. Out in the casino for everyone to see, at least." His eyes sparkled with amusement.

"You don't have shareholders, though, so what does it matter how things look? It's not like you have to hide the fact that we've met from your father. He's the only one who can greenlight the acquisition, and it seems to me like he's trying to get you on board."

"He is, and I'm lucky he's still listening to me, but it's not him I'm worried about. I can't remember when I last spent time with a woman and didn't see photographs or hear about it the next day. Any time I date someone, it's news almost immediately, and tabloids rarely follow up to see if their information is correct. Morgan Enterprises doesn't have shareholders, but our employees are sure to catch wind of it if I'm seen meeting with you. Some of them already know that Saffron wants to acquire us, and they panic. They worry about their positions with the company, and it fractures their focus. It's not good for anyone."

"I see." It made perfect sense, but that didn't dampen her attraction for Richard. She shifted in her seat, feeling uneasy.

He pulled a packet of candies out of his jacket pocket. "Would you like a Millie?" He held the packet out to her.

She had always loved Millies. The lemon- and ginger-flavored hard candies were the oldest and one of the bestselling products Morgan Confectioners produced. She accepted one from the packet and popped it in her mouth. "I do love Millies. I'd like to see something like them for Saffron, once we expand beyond chocolate." She relaxed as the flavor filled her mouth. Like every other kid growing up, she had loved candy. When she was a teenager undergoing chemotherapy, though, there were days when hard candy was all she could tolerate. During the days when nausea was a constant companion, she went through Millies by the case. The lemon and ginger combination was a soothing balm for her then, and she still found a great deal of comfort in the familiar flavors now.

"They were my mother's favorite. They're named after her, you know." Richard popped one in his own mouth and tucked the packet back into his pocket.

"Your mother's name was Millie?" She raised her eyebrows. As much as his family history had been public knowledge, she could not remember learning his mother's name.

"Well, Millie is short for Amelia. My father always called her Millie, and she loved these candies, so he named them after her. It was the first candy Morgan ever sold."

"Made with love, I guess. Maybe that's why they're such a success."

"Morgan products are more likely to have a story than not. We don't just mass-produce things without putting thought into the entire line. That's why I'm so hesitant to partner with other companies or allow any of our divisions to be bought out by bigger corporations. Morgan isn't just a job for me."

"It's your life, your legacy. I see that, but surely exploring other options doesn't mean you don't care for the company." Back on familiar ground, her confidence returned. If she focused on business, on her work, she could ignore the hypnotic green of his eyes.

"If we sell a division to Saffron, then that sets a precedent. Every other division or product line will be seen as up for grabs at worst, and at best it makes us look weak. This company means more to me than anything. My father built Morgan Confectioners from the ground up. The fact that I've been on board to see the rest of Morgan Enterprises come to fruition has been the greatest gift, and I don't take it for granted."

"I remember reading a story in a magazine about the first candy shop your family opened. There was even an old picture of all of you. You were such a cute kid."

"Any time you wonder if there's a chance that I'll change my mind, think of that picture. That's how I see all of Morgan Enterprises. It literally represents everything I love, and I won't discount it. My brother and I spent our childhood in that shop.

He's moved on to other things, but I'm not letting it go for anything."

She knew that Michael Morgan started the candy company from scratch, but it wasn't as though he were a bootstrap entrepreneur. The Morgans started out with plenty of money. He just managed to hit on a brilliant business idea at the right time. The family fortune went back much further than Michael. If the entirety of Morgan Enterprises folded, they would likely still be quite comfortable financially. Richard's passion for the family business was unexpected. She had him pegged as a savvy businessman, someone who protected his wealth, but this went further than money. Sussing out his true motivation made her job even harder. Saffron had nothing besides money to offer, and it was becoming clear to her that Richard Morgan was not a man who could be bought.

"If Saffron acquired your confections division, I would do my best to maintain the standards of quality and innovation your brand is known for. With Saffron's funding and focus behind the line, it could only get better. I can absolutely promise you that I'd do everything in my power to make it as painless as possible for you to let it go." It was a small concession, but it was all she could offer. Her mission wouldn't change just because she understood his hesitation.

"I plan to do everything in my power to prevent ever having to rely on that promise." Richard was calm, pleasant enough, but the steely look in his eyes told her she'd be in for a fight if she moved forward. "Once we land, it's back to business as usual as far as I'm concerned."

"So we'll go our separate ways and pretend this weekend never happened?" It would be a shame to never again find her way into Richard's bed, but it was for the best.

"I don't see any way around it. We want different things and as appealing as I find you," he swept an open gaze up and down the length of her body, "we have to keep our distance. That's all there is to it."

"Well, then it was fun while it lasted. Just know that I'm not going to stop trying to get what I want." Her determination was rock-solid, but she softened her tone with a smile. "I'm sure you understand."

"I do, and I'm sure you understand that I won't give an inch on this."

She finished her drink and gave him a cool smile. "Then I guess we're on the same page."

Chapter Five

Her acquisitions team sat around a mahogany conference table, the air conditioning whirring softly in the background and very nearly lulling Yvette to sleep. Nothing had been the same since that one crazy night three weeks ago. Anything could set her imagination off, the mention of Las Vegas, seeing Morgan Confectioners candies on store shelves, catching the scent of soap. Soap. If she closed her eyes, she could almost feel his hands on her, sliding over her curves, covering every inch of her body in that shower. Steam floated around them as hot water pelted her back, exotic fragrances swirled around them in the thick air.

"Yvette?" Her department head's voice drifted into her consciousness, clearing the steam and toppling her out of her little fantasy. The woman at the head of the table stared at her over the tops of her eyeglasses, an annoyed look on her face.

Had she fallen asleep? Was she drooling? Did she make an embarrassing noise? She refilled her glass with ice water and took a long drink, determined to wake up and focus. She straightened her charcoal pencil skirt over her thighs and sat up straight as she turned her attention to the table.

Clearing her throat, she attempted her most professional, competent tone. "I'm sorry. What was that?"

Her co-workers tittered, and a hot flush crept into her cheeks. A quick swipe across her face assured her that she hadn't been drooling. Summoning her inner professional, she faced the department head and listened intently. "Yvette, I was just asking you for an update on the Morgan Confectioners progress. The last time you briefed us, you'd met with Michael Morgan, but that was before the conference. Anything new to report? Have you made any headway?"

Anything new? You could say that. "I was able to meet Richard Morgan informally in Vegas, but he's adamantly opposed to our proposal. I believe that he has a great deal of influence over his father's decision-making, but ultimately, Michael Morgan still has the final say. At this point, we might consider reviewing our strategy to strengthen our position. It doesn't seem likely to pass if Richard has anything to say about it."

"Have you made contact with anyone at Morgan since your meeting with Richard?"

Yvette hesitated. Not only had she agreed that she and Richard would keep their distance, but after hearing him speak so passionately of his devotion to the company, she wasn't as inclined to absorb it into Saffron. He cared for Morgan Confectioners in a way nobody else ever could. It was part of his history, a tie to both his childhood and his mother, something knitted into the fabric of his soul. Trying to convince him to give it up now felt wrong and ugly—almost predatory.

"I sent brief notes to both Michael and Richard to thank them for meeting with me and to keep the door open for future discussion." She scanned her calendar. "Let's see, that was a little over three weeks ago, and I haven't heard from either of them. It's my opinion that we need to revisit our game plan. Any further attempts to engage them will likely be seen as intrusive. They have our complete offer. If I contact them again before they respond, I'll just be repeating myself."

Her boss's eyes narrowed. "So what you're telling me is that it's been almost a month since you've made any kind of progress on this account?"

Yvette shifted uncomfortably, but spoke firmly. "I felt that until we have something new to discuss, continuing to contact the Morgans would not be well-received. I think it would be wise for me to meet with the mergers and acquisitions team to freshen our strategy before approaching them again."

"Very well. I'd like to see something on the calendar immediately. The longer this drags out, the less likely we are to come to an agreement."

"I also think we should have a tentative list of alternative companies ready for research, should the Morgans ultimately turn us down." Yvette would do her job, would approach this assignment with the same professionalism as any other account, but she knew more about the players than usual. How much could she reveal about Richard's motivations without compromising herself?

The department head looked irritated, but agreed. "Fine. Compile it and send it to my office. I'll keep it until our attempts with Morgan Confectioners are exhausted."

Grateful to be out of the hot seat, Yvette gathered her files and calendar, ready to disappear into her office. The hint of a nagging thought persisted, but she couldn't put her finger on it. Tate, her assistant, met her in the hallway as she left the meeting, pressing message slips into her hand and briefing her on new developments. She listened with half of her attention, searching her brain for the source of the nagging thought as they strode down the hall towards her office. He continued to talk and set a stack of folders on her desk as she sat down.

"Would you bring me a coffee? I'm never going to make it through the afternoon at this rate." She smiled up at Tate from her desk chair, determined to focus. He nodded and disappeared from the doorway, leaving her alone in the silent office.

Soft sunlight filtered in between the slats of her blinds, and the muted chatter and bustling of a busy workday beyond her walls floated through the room. Yvette had created her office space with such care, wanting to project an image that was both professional and welcoming. Some of her male colleagues decorated their offices as though they were reliving their college days, with basketball nets attached to doors and toys littering their shelves. She wondered how something similar would go over in her office, if she hung posters reflecting her teen interests or had dolls perched on her shelves. The playing field would never be level, and she had to make her peace with that, had to protect her professional image in a way her male colleagues didn't. Her office space urged people to come in, to sit and stay while she worked her magic. The artwork was pleasing, soothing, and her candy dishes were always full. The plush chairs sitting opposite her desk tended to lull visitors into relaxation while she spoke, making them more amenable to her requests.

Tate returned with her coffee, fixed exactly the way she liked it, and she wrapped her hands around the warm mug. "Thank you so much, you're a lifesaver. I was drifting off in the meeting and will never make it through the afternoon without a little caffeine."

"You got it. Is there anything else?"

She knew there was something she was missing but simply couldn't think of it. "No, I guess that's it for now. Thank you."

Left alone, she sipped her coffee, expecting to savor it and enjoy the aroma. Instead, nausea gripped her and she reached for the small garbage can at the side of her desk. A couple of deep breaths and a moment later, the urge subsided and she sat back in her chair, grateful that she hadn't been sick in the conference room. She needed sleep, and badly. Since the trip to Vegas, stress had been her constant companion, and sleep eluded her, which likely explained the drowsiness and nausea. She never felt well when she missed too much sleep. Between failing to close the deal with Morgan Confectioners and succumbing to her lust for Richard like some kind of hormone-crazed teenager, it felt like she was losing control of her life. Like she was someone else lately.

Pushing the coffee cup away, she pulled out her calendar, prepared to tackle her work with renewed enthusiasm, to regain her sense of competency. Ready to put thoughts of Richard behind her and focus on things she could control, she jiggled her mouse to wake up her computer. As she scanned the dates on her calendar, noting meetings and deadlines, the nagging thought that she was missing something resurfaced, then crystallized. Her period was late.

She was never late; this couldn't be. It was only a week, but it was late enough to set off alarm bells. Her radiation treatments had made it impossible for her to become pregnant, hadn't they? But she'd never been this late before. Best to find out for sure. Nothing would be accomplished until she knew, so she left early and headed for the nearest drugstore.

• • •

Richard held a finger up as his assistant, Chloe, leaned around his doorframe. The conference call was winding down, but he had asked for no interruptions and her impertinence irritated him. She bit her lip nervously and stepped inside the office, closing the door silently behind her. She shifted from one leg to another, obviously waiting for an opportunity to relay some urgent message. He finished his call without rushing, sat back in his chair, and spread his hands before him.

"Yes, Chloe, what is it?" He didn't bother to keep the irritation out of his voice.

"Sir, Yvette Cruz from Saffron Sweets is here to see you. I told her that you were unavailable, but she insists that she speak to you. I don't think she'll leave." Chloe glanced at the door, looking ready to dart out.

He sat up. "She's here?"

Chloe nodded and took a step back. Yvette had honored their agreement of no contact for almost a month after they said goodbye at the airport. She hadn't so much as emailed him about the acquisition. During that time, he had made it his mission to eradicate all thoughts of Yvette Cruz from his mind. By burying himself in work and spending any free time he had left over at the gym, he told himself he had managed to release the memories of that night. He had almost forgotten the way her skin felt beneath his hands, the exquisite pleasure he took in unpinning her hair and watching it shake loose around her slim shoulders, and the unbearably satisfying weight of her perfect breasts in his hands. He told himself that he could scarcely remember her delectable vanilla scent, the taste of her on his tongue, the delicious sound of her throaty laugh. No, she was a threat to his business and he didn't want any part of her. Not even her shapely curves, her lush backside, or the exquisite depths of her mouth. Yvette Cruz was officially off his radar as far as he was concerned, so when the phone calls started coming from her office last week, his assistant was given strict orders to refuse all her efforts to connect.

"What does she want?"

"She won't say, sir. She'll only speak directly to you." Chloe seemed stuck between following Richard's directives and admitting Yvette to his office just to put an end to the uncomfortable tension.

He briefly considered having Yvette removed by security, but that seemed a bit extreme. Besides, he doubted that even that would dissuade her. She was clearly a woman on a mission, and he could make her leave today, but she'd surely continue to return until she got her audience. He refused to admit that a part of him wanted to see her again, longed for one more night with her even.

He sighed; what good was an assistant who couldn't even keep unwanted visitors from darkening his doorstep? Having seen Yvette in action, though, he knew that Chloe was no match for her. She had won him over when he was determined to stay far away from her after all, and he wasn't a man who was easily persuaded. Might as well see her and get it over with.

"Fine, see her in." Surely the surge of adrenaline was his body's way of preparing for potential battle, not anything to do with attraction.

Visibly relieved to be dismissed without further discussion, Chloe scurried out of the office so fast she nearly tripped over her own feet. Yvette walked in, and he could instantly tell that this wasn't a professional visit. Something was different about her. The confident gleam in her eyes was gone; the sexy sashay was missing from her step. She was still achingly beautiful, reminding him of an exotic jewel in the crimson dress so fitted it could have been painted on her delicate frame, but there was more. Something in her had changed, and he saw a vulnerability that hadn't been there before.

"Come on in and have a seat." He indicated the chairs in front of his desk and watched as she crossed the room to sit down. She seemed to be carrying herself differently. The change was probably indiscernible to most people. Most people weren't as unwittingly attuned to her as he was, though. Most people didn't spend days and nights distracted by thoughts of her.

"I'm sorry for barging in like this, but you haven't returned any of my calls." She held her head high, and her voice was clear and confident.

"We have nothing more to talk about. Our agreement was to have no further contact. I thought you understood my reasoning, even if you didn't agree with it. As much as I enjoyed our time together, we simply can't be together." He was thankful for his desk, glad to have a solid barrier between them. He wanted nothing more than to reach out and touch her, and that would most certainly send a mixed message.

"I realize that—"

He held up a hand to cut her off. "I can't stop my father from taking meetings with you, but I was dead serious when I said that I would do everything within my power to keep him from selling to Saffron. There's nothing that will convince me to change my mind. Quite frankly, I'm surprised that you would go to such lengths to continue on this course."

"I haven't met with Michael again. I need to speak with you, and only you." Her increasing frustration was evident. Her eyes flashed in irritation, her gorgeous mouth was set in an impatient line. She was sexy even when she was flustered.

"Like I said, there's nothing more for us to discuss. I'm sorry that you came all the way over here, but my assistant will see you out." He leaned over his desk to buzz Chloe. He needed to get her out of here before he gave in to the desire to keep her close to him.

"I'm pregnant!"

Richard stopped, his hand frozen in midair above the phone. For a moment, time stopped, and he was chilled to his toes. Realizing that his mouth was agape and his hand was hovering over his desk, he relaxed and took a beat to compose himself. "Congratulations."

"It's yours." She sat back in her chair and watched for his reaction.

"What?" He sputtered. "I used a condom!" Not many things ruffled or even surprised him, but this was a first. The news coupled with her potent effect on him shifted his balance and disrupted his usual calm competency.

"Sure, the first time, but not after that. Listen, I know that this is a shock. It was for me too, so I don't expect you to process this immediately. I certainly didn't."

"Didn't you tell me you can't get pregnant? How do you know it's mine? How can you even be sure this soon?" He heard his voice climb by at least an octave, and he knew he sounded as panicky as he felt. With great effort, Richard calmed himself down. He would handle this news like he handled everything else, with authority.

"I haven't been with anyone else, that's how I know. You're the father, and there's no doubt about it. Until it happened, I truly thought that I couldn't get pregnant after my radiation. I thought that motherhood was the one dream I'd have to let go, and I thought that I had, but then—" she paused. "I was having all these symptoms, and it started adding up once I checked the calendar. I finally decided to take the pregnancy test just to rule it out, even though I didn't think anything would come of it. If I hadn't caught it early it could have been weeks before I noticed, since that was the last thing I expected. The possibility of pregnancy wasn't even on my radar. I honestly was as surprised as you are, and quite frankly, this is nothing short of a miracle as far as I'm concerned." Her eyes shone under the office fluorescents, and her hands were clasped tightly in her lap, her knuckles white.

"Well, what do you need? Do you need money?" He scraped a hand across his chin, realizing too late how heartless he sounded. He needed to put an end to his spiral towards panic, but his tone was bordering on cruel, and that was wrong. This was a surprise, but he wasn't the kind of man who treated news of this gravity with such callousness. Richard gave himself a mental shake and cleared his head. He was not this kind of man. Her lip quivered almost imperceptibly, and he regretted the casual dismissal in his tone even more. She was a corporate threat, but if he were honest with himself, she wasn't the seductive danger that he previously assumed her to be. She wasn't an actual enemy; it was just in his best interest to stay far away from her. He rose and walked around his desk to take the seat next to her.

"I'm sorry." His voice was softer, more relaxed now that he was placing himself in familiar territory. Fixing problems was what he did best. "I spoke before processing the news. Just tell me what you need, and it's yours. I want to help however I can. If it's money, consider it done."

Yvette leaned away from him and stiffened, eyes blazing. "I don't want your money. I don't need anything from you." Her voice dripped with disdain. "I'm keeping the baby, regardless of how it will break my parents' hearts that I'm going to be an unwed mother. It'll kill them when I tell them what's happened, but it's better than the alternative."

"Again, I apologize. I just assumed … "

"You assumed because you think you know me, but you don't. You assumed because you think I'm something that I'm not. I'm not interested in your money, and I'm not trying to use the baby to get anything from you. I didn't come to you for help in getting rid of my problem." She practically spit the words at him. "I came to you because you have the right to know that you're going to be a father, and what you do with that information is your decision. I realize that you weren't planning this, and you don't have a say in it. You can waive your rights if that's what you want, and you'll never hear from me again. You don't have to do anything or even be involved at all." She was full of righteous indignation now, and Richard sensed that there was little he could say to endear himself to her. Time for damage control.

"Okay, so you're keeping the baby. I didn't realize that you were so traditional, and again, I apologize, but … do you even want to be a mother?" Her career had to be as demanding as his. How did she plan on managing motherhood on her own?

"I never dreamed that I'd have this chance, and I certainly never thought I'd end up having a baby with someone I'm not even involved with, but it is what it is. I honestly thought that motherhood wasn't in the cards for me, so I'm embracing this as the gift that it is. I'll figure everything out somehow, with or without you."

Yvette was going to have his baby and raise him or her on her own? She wasn't even considering … alternatives? Her family must be much more traditional than he would have guessed. He could only imagine his own father's delight at the news that he'd be a grandfather.

He'd probably dote on the child, thrilled that the Morgan legacy would continue after all. *Legacy.* The deal. Everything he wanted wrapped up in one neat package. He'd have the company he loved and the family he'd always wanted. Ignoring the nagging thought that he would surely go to hell for even considering it, he blurted out, "Let's get married then."

Yvette's brown eyes widened, and her mouth formed into the perfect "O" of surprise that he had seen that morning he'd joined her in the shower. The morning he now knew was when they could have conceived their baby. "What? You want to get married?"

"If it is, in fact, my baby, then yes. I don't want an illegitimate child any more than you do."

"How romantic." She stopped just short of rolling her eyes at him.

"You came to me with a practical problem, and I offered a practical solution." He spread his hands and inclined his head. And if his solution happened to give him control of the confections division, then that was just a bonus. "Surely being with me is preferable to going this alone."

"I don't consider my child to be a problem." She sat up straighter, her voice heavy.

"Not the child, but the circumstances surrounding your pregnancy certainly seem to trouble you. If your family is as traditional as you say, this news will not go over well. Getting married will solve that problem."

"I'm sorry, but I just don't see how this is a good idea." She shook her head and shifted her eyes away from his gaze.

"How could it not be? You and I are having a baby together. What could be wrong about creating a family for him to be born into? People marry for much less all the time."

"Him?" One of her eyebrows quirked up and the smallest hint of amusement lit in her eyes.

"What?"

"Him. You said him. As in, the baby will be a boy, and you will have a son." The ghost of a smile flitted across her mouth and gave him the encouragement to forge ahead.

"Or her. Either one. What do you think?" She really was lovely when she smiled. She would be lovely as the pregnancy changed her body, too. He could picture her curves softening, filling out and growing along with the baby inside of her. His baby. A little boy to carry his name or a little girl who looked just like her beautiful mother. He'd never considered trying marriage again, after the pain and humiliation Chelsea had put him through, but this was different. This time there was a common bond beyond emotions, something his first marriage was sorely lacking: a child. With the baby, he'd have the traditional family he so desperately wanted.

"I think I should take some time to think about it." Her voice was soft, the anger and irritation gone, replaced with a sadness he couldn't place.

Sensing an outright refusal was imminent, he slid out of his chair and onto his knee. He took her hand in his and looked into her eyes, reminded once again of sweet melted chocolate. She really did seem sweet, nothing at all like the ruthless seductress he had once taken her for. Marrying Yvette would give him everything he had ever wanted. He'd be in complete control of the company that he loved. He'd have a beautiful wife and a child, an heir. The beautiful wife might not have been in his original plans, but if he had to marry again, then he could do worse than Yvette. Creating a family was a compelling reason to take the chance on another marriage.

"Yvette Cruz, will you marry me?" He did his best to look charming and gave her an open smile. It faded a bit when she failed to answer right away.

Silence stretched between them, thick with anticipation and tension. She shook her head sadly, and a single tear slid down her cheek. "No."

She extracted her hands from his and stood. As she swiped the back of her hand across her cheek, she looked down at him.

"This is not at all what I expected. I never wanted to be an unwed mother, and it will just kill my parents, but I'm not sure I'm willing to bring a child into a loveless marriage."

He stood and took her hand in his. "A loveless marriage? That sounds pretty harsh."

"You know what I mean. We don't really know each other, and less than a month ago you actively disliked me." Tears fell down her cheeks and she brushed them away.

"True, but that was then. I didn't know you, and I was simply trying to protect the company. Things are different now, much different. The baby changes everything." He pulled her closer, lowered his voice, and tried to bring her back around.

"I need time to think things through. I never thought I would find myself in this position, and marriage isn't something I take lightly. To me, it's a lifelong commitment, so you'll forgive me if I consider it from every angle before I agree." She sniffled and wiped the tears from her cheeks, and straightened her spine, holding her head high.

Richard released her hand and pressed a kiss to her forehead. He breathed in the clean fragrance of her hair before moving back and looking into her eyes. "Take all the time you need. I'll be here for you whatever you decide, and I intend to be a part of this child's life. You won't be alone in this."

"Thank you Richard. I'll be in touch." She turned on her heel and walked out, leaving him alone in his office. He stood frozen in place, unsure what to do next for the first time in a long time.

•••

Yvette paced the length of her living room, certain she would wear a hole in the carpet if her younger sister didn't arrive soon. She looked to the anniversary clock she'd inherited from her grandmother. Veronica should be here any minute. With every tick of the clock, she grew more nervous, knowing that facing her family with the news would be the hardest thing she'd ever had to do. Things with Richard were complicated, but telling him about the baby had gone much better than she dared hope. The marriage proposal was a surprise. Should she have said yes? Being a single mother wasn't her first choice, but it wasn't as shameful as her family would likely think. Surely with time they would come to accept her choice, wouldn't they? Still, bringing the baby into a family where she was married to the father might not be the worst idea.

Blessedly, Veronica finally arrived, walking in the front door without knocking, her head down as she typed out a text on her phone. Still not looking up, she dropped her handbag on a table in the foyer and crossed the room to meet Yvette before setting her phone down on the coffee table.

Veronica dropped down onto the couch and looked to Yvette. "Hey, I got here as fast as I could. What's going on?"

Yvette sat in a wingback chair opposite the couch and folded her hands in her lap, took a deep breath, and faced her younger sister. "No sense in beating around the bush. I'm pregnant."

It felt good to say it out loud to someone other than Richard. Her family was so conservative and traditional that she'd dreaded the moment they'd find out. Their strict Catholic faith meant that it didn't matter that she was an adult. All that mattered was that she was pregnant out of holy wedlock. Her sister was not as intimidating as her parents, but it wasn't easy to admit what had happened. Maybe by the time she told her parents, she'd be more comfortable sharing the news. Baby steps, she thought ironically.

Her sister sputtered, the news taking a while to process. "What? You know, for some reason I thought you couldn't even get pregnant. Did I make that up?"

"No, I thought the radiation made me infertile, but apparently I was wrong. I can definitely get pregnant." A nervous laugh bubbled up.

Her sister's eyes were wide with surprise, but there was no judgment in her expression. "I didn't even know you were seeing anyone."

"I haven't been, not really." She twisted her hands in her lap. Veronica wasn't judging her for getting pregnant, but her opinion might change once she discovered that it was the result of a wild one-night stand.

"What?" Veronica kicked off her shoes and pulled her feet up onto the couch. Propping her elbows on her knees, she sat forward, as though she were settling in for a juicy gossip session. "Then who's the father? Do you even know?"

"Of course I know who it is! I had a kind of … fling when I went to Vegas for that conference." It sounded tawdry when she said it out loud.

"Oh, so is it a guy from work, some candy guy?" She snapped her finger. "It's not some random guy from Vegas, is it?"

"No, nothing like that. He's someone who lives here. It's just complicated." She chewed on her bottom lip. The further she went in explanation, the more twisted the situation appeared.

"Complicated how? Who is it?" Veronica practically vibrated with curiosity.

Yvette looked at the floor, avoiding eye contact for a moment, as she acknowledged that the mess went further than just an unplanned pregnancy. "It's Richard Morgan."

Veronica sat back dramatically, her mouth hanging open. "Richard Morgan, the millionaire? The hot, single millionaire? That Richard Morgan?"

"That's the one." Despite herself, Yvette smiled. Her sister did have a flair for the dramatic.

"How did this happen? How do you two even know each other?" Yvette's fears of judgment disappeared with her sister's enthusiasm. From the outside, it probably appeared that she'd made quite the catch.

"My company is trying to buy Morgan's confections division, and I've been in charge of the account. Up until that night, we'd never even met, and he didn't even seem to like me very much when we did. We spent some time together at the conference, and things kind of just got out of hand. After that one night, we agreed not to see each other again, because of the business and how quickly rumors spread, but then this came up."

"Wow. I wouldn't mind letting things get out of hand with him." Veronica waggled her eyebrows comically. "If you know what I mean."

"Hey! That's the father of my child you're talking about." Yvette smiled a little, though. Her parents were going to be tough, but telling her sister made it seem like things weren't so insurmountable. Saying it out loud and not facing harsh judgment relaxed her as much as she'd hoped it would.

"Have you told him?" Her sister asked, more serious now.

"Yeah, I went by his office and told him. Now things are even more complicated. I wasn't sure if he'd be angry, or demand a paternity test, or something worse. I thought that he might think I tricked him, or that I was after his money, who knows. I couldn't have predicted his reaction in a million years though, because he proposed."

"What? Oh my gosh!" Veronica squealed and hugged a throw pillow to her chest.

"Sorry to disappoint you, but I said no."

"Why? He's the father of your baby, he's rich, and he's hot— like Channing Tatum-dipped-in-chocolate hot. Why would you turn him down?"

"Because we're not in love and he just proposed because I'm pregnant. If this hadn't happened, we wouldn't have ever seen each other again outside of business. Probably not even for that, if he had any say in it."

Veronica folded her hands in her lap, her expression concerned and serious. Not a hint of the joking, drama queen remained. "You could grow to love each other, and people get married all the time for far less important reasons. Being married to the father of your child isn't a bad idea." Their parents had drilled the importance of marriage and family into them, and Veronica obviously absorbed the lesson. Being young and not as traditional didn't mean she wasn't still a good Catholic daughter.

"I don't think marrying a virtual stranger is such a great idea either, regardless of how we were brought up."

"Speaking of our upbringing, how are you going to tell Mom and Dad?"

Yvette sighed. Telling her parents was going to be tough, and Veronica's reaction confirmed it. "I don't know. I think I might just suck it up and call them. I can't keep it from them, so I might as well get it over with."

"Yep, like pulling off a bandage, quick and painful, but over in a flash. I can be with you when you tell them if you want."

"I can handle it, but thanks. I'll probably need support afterwards. I'm sure they'll freak out."

"Without a doubt. You know, I love you no matter what and I don't judge you for this, but they really are going to take it hard. After everything they've done for us, so that we could have the life we had, this is going to be tough. Really tough. I can already picture Dad yelling about how he didn't work three jobs to put you through college so you could get pregnant out of wedlock. You should prepare for the worst."

Yvette chewed on her bottom lip. "I know. I feel horrible about how disappointed they're going to be, like I let them down. No matter what else I do in life, this is going to trump everything with them. I'm afraid it's going to be like nothing else matters but this one big mistake."

"I hate to say it, but you're probably right—for Dad at least. Mom will probably be upset but understanding. She'll come around before he does, and she might even help him get through it. She doesn't think you're still twelve years old like Dad seems to. You might want to remind him that you're twenty-seven." Veronica laughed, short and sympathetic. "Not that it will make a difference to him."

"I wonder if I should try to make him see that it's not the end of the world, or if I should just let him go off and wait until his rant ends. Oh, this is so hard." She dropped her head into her hands and puffed out a sharp breath. "All right, I'm going to call them tonight. Putting it off and obsessing about it won't make it any easier. No need to postpone the inevitable." Once she told them over the phone, chances were good that they'd hop in the car and leave their home in Reading to confront her in person.

Veronica stood and hooked her purse over her shoulder. "Okay, just call me if you need anything. Actually, call me after you talk to them regardless. I want to hear how it goes."

Yvette watched as her sister crossed the living room. "I will. Wish me luck."

"Good luck," Veronica said as she spared her one last, sympathetic look before opening the door. "You're going to need it."

Chapter Six

A full week and a dozen unreturned phone calls from Richard later, Yvette dozed on the pink velvet chaise in her glass-ceilinged library. It was always her favorite room in the house, but never more so than during a thunderstorm. Few things were cozier than curling up inside, safe from the raging weather outside the windows. Rain pelted the panes, and lightning lit up the early evening sky. A pregnancy book lay on the floor, dropped as she drifted off into sleep. She was dreaming, reliving Richard's proposal, only this time her response was to throw herself into his embrace and whisper "yes." A chime sounded in the distance and pulled her from her light sleep. The doorbell.

Yvette sat up and looked around the room, blinking, orienting herself. She padded through the darkened rooms of her house, flipping on lights along the way, and peered through the peephole. Her father stood in front of her door, grim-faced and wet from the rain. Yvette unlocked the deadbolt and opened the door, her heart in her stomach.

"Dad." Tears sprang to her eyes, and she swallowed against the lump forming in her throat. Her father made no move to greet her or take her in his arms like she wanted, so she stepped aside to let him enter. She craned her neck around the corner to look for her mother.

"Your mother is in the car. Your Aunt Celia called as we pulled into your neighborhood." His tone was clipped, telling her this wouldn't be a friendly visit. She didn't expect anything different, but it stung.

She had worried this would happen, that her parents would show up at her doorstep unannounced and barge into her life. The hour-long drive from the neighborhood where she grew up wouldn't deter them, not when she'd disappointed them so gravely. Their phone conversation a couple of days ago had been just as tense and uncomfortable as she had feared. Telling her parents that she was pregnant was easily the most difficult conversation she had ever had. By the time she could finally hang up, her father's steely silence was worse than if he had just yelled at her. She could feel their disappointment rolling across the miles, could tell that regardless of her age, they considered having an unwed mother for a child to be a monumental shame.

Living miles away from her childhood home, busy with her professional life, Yvette could sometimes forget her conservative, traditional Catholic upbringing. Her parents hadn't left their heritage or their beliefs behind when they moved to Pennsylvania from Puerto Rico. If anything, it became stronger as they wove their way into the fabric of their largely Puerto Rican neighborhood. She saw herself as an independent adult with a life of her own, someone who was moral without being perfect. Her parents' black-and-white views were overwhelming, and as much as she sought to evolve, they were a part of who she was. Who she always would be, even if, to her, an unintended pregnancy wasn't the unspeakable shame that her parents saw. She knew that she could raise the baby on her own, could even develop a healthy relationship with Richard, eventually. To her parents, though, this would never be enough. They'd want a marriage or they'd consider themselves failures as parents. The sad look in her father's eyes now confirmed what she knew to be true. He couldn't accept this.

Her mother bustled up the walkway and into Yvette's foyer, her face full of concern and sadness. "Oh, *mija*. Come here." She pulled Yvette into a fierce hug that smelled like Pine Sol and home, and her oversized tote bag bounced against their hips. Yvette melted into the embrace, allowing herself a brief moment when everything was going to be all right. At least her mother wasn't angry with her. Anger would have been easier to swallow, though. The disappointment she saw reflected in their expressions cut to the heart. She blinked against the tears forming in her eyes and took a deep, shuddering breath. Yvette pulled away and led her parents into the living room where they settled themselves on her sofa. Taking a seat opposite from them on her plush wingback chair, she gave them what she hoped was a calm, mature look, the same one she used during difficult meetings at work. The look of a woman who didn't need her parents riding into town to fix her problems, one who was more than old enough to make her own decisions. "You didn't need to drive all the way out here."

"We needed to see for ourselves that you are okay." Her mother's voice was soft and filled with sadness.

"I'm fine. Everything's fine." Yvette held her head high and willed back her tears. Why could she handle anything that came her way professionally with aplomb, but when it came to facing her parents she was suddenly twelve years old again?

"How can you say that? My daughter, my little girl, pregnant and unmarried! This is not fine! This is far from fine!" Her father started to rise but sat back at his wife's gentle hand on his shoulder. The disappointment and hurt in his eyes broke Yvette's heart. "This is not how we raised you, and this is not what we want for you. I didn't sacrifice so much to give you everything only to have you throw it back in my face."

She'd known they wouldn't approve, but she hadn't anticipated her father seeing her pregnancy as an affront to the sacrifices he made to give her a good life. Her father had moved her mother to America from Puerto Rico when they were newlyweds so their children could be born here, into the land of possibilities and opportunities. He'd left family and friends behind to start over, just for them. There had been years during her childhood when he worked two jobs just to keep the family fed, and thinking back on his commitment to her, on his sacrifices, she wished she'd said yes to Richard's proposal. Giving her father the comfort of an engagement was a small price to pay.

"Dad, that's the thing. This happening doesn't mean that I don't appreciate everything you've done for me. I will always be grateful for everything you did for me, truly, but I'm not a little girl, and I will be fine. I can handle everything, and I will. I'm sorry to have disappointed you, but it's going to be okay. I just don't want ... " The doorbell chimed and she looked towards the foyer. Her parents exchanged a tense look as she rose, confused, and walked to the door.

Richard stood in her doorway, his hair damp from the rain. She stepped back to let him inside, surprised enough to blurt, "What are you doing here? What's going on?"

Before he could answer, her father walked into the foyer. "I called him and told him to meet us here. I needed to see him for myself and give him the chance to answer for what he's done and make things right." A stern look on his face, it was clear he was unashamed that he'd meddled. "When you told me that this candy man was the father of your baby, I looked him up. He wasn't hard to find." He sneered as he said the words. She would have laughed at the absurdity of the situation, at her father's self-righteous look, but it was just too surreal.

"Dad, seriously. He hasn't done anything to answer for. We are two consenting adults, and I'm sorry that you're so disappointed, but I can handle this myself." She could feel her face burning with embarrassment.

"Yvette Isabella Cruz, I am your father and until you are married, you are under my protection. I must do what I think is right."

Richard looked much too relaxed amidst the tension in the room. Was there a situation he couldn't handle? As things with her parents spiraled out of control, she was actually glad to see him, happy to have his competent, calming presence. "Hector, Elisa, hello. It's nice to meet you in person." He lowered his voice and inclined his head so that his lips were almost touching Yvette's ear, sending warm breath across her neck. "Can we speak somewhere privately?"

"Ah, sure, let's do that." She looked to her parents, sitting straight-backed and stern on her couch. Was she the only one ruffled by the situation? Her father looked positively smug, having brought the man who sullied his pristine daughter to answer for his actions. "Come with me. We can go to my library and speak privately."

She led him into her library and closed the door behind them. Rain pelted the glass ceiling, her reading lamp gave the room a cozy glow, and Yvette wished more than anything that everyone would just leave so she could crawl back into her cocoon and dream. The library was her sanctuary, now more than ever. The pregnancy and the stress surrounding it had worn her out, with more afternoons finding her nodding off at her desk than not. Richard wandered the perimeter of the library, lightly running his fingertips over book spines, until he stopped in front of a shelf. He took a framed picture and held it out to her.

"Is this your sister?"

"Nope, that's me."

His confusion was sweet and oddly endearing since he was so rarely surprised. She was accustomed to the double take people did when they saw older pictures of her, but it was especially enjoyable to catch Richard off guard. The picture he held was one of a teenaged Yvette, fifty pounds heavier, wearing braces and unfashionable glasses, with skin that brought pizza toppings to mind. He looked from the picture to her, back again, and a tiny ping of understanding lit up his eyes. She'd seen that look before too, but it was usually with women. That was the look that said he understood why her clothes were couture, why her hair and makeup were always flawless, why accessories mattered to her. She had spent so long as the ugly duckling and had decided it was time to enjoy being the beautiful swan. As her cancer treatment progressed, losing weight was the last thing on her mind, but it was a fortunate side effect. Once she was safely in remission, the weight didn't return and she took advantage of her second chance to capitalize on her natural beauty by perfecting her makeup techniques and learning what clothing worked best for her body. Determined to never go back to the chubby, plain girl she once was, she learned about healthy diet and exercise and was able to maintain her weight.

"So, I guess you know why I'm here," he began.

"I can't believe my father actually called you. He will never accept that I'm an adult, that he doesn't have a say over everything that goes on in my life." A soft blanket sat at the foot of her chaise, and she thought it would be perfect to hide beneath.

"Oh, I got quite an earful." To her relief, Richard laughed. "It was hard for me to get a word in edgewise, not that he would've listened if I had. He talked so fast it actually took me a minute to figure out who he was and why he was calling me. It was very confusing."

"Oh God, I'm so sorry." Her words were muffled as she covered her face with her hands. It was one thing for her family to swoop in and micromanage her life. It was another for her father to manipulate Richard.

He set the picture back on the shelf and crossed the room to pull her into a loose embrace. She stiffened at the contact, but relinquished control when he continued to hold her. All the emotions, the uncertainty, the drama had her exhausted. She was tired of pushing him away, tired of keeping him at a distance. Most of all, she was tired of shouldering everything alone. It was time to relent and let him comfort her. At his gentle touch, she melted against his body, grateful for its warmth and stability.

Richard brushed his lips across the top of her head and pulled away enough to look her in the eye. "It's fine. He was a little over the top, but I understand. You're his little girl and he's just worried about you. Let's sit." He took her hand and led her to a pair of lavender wingback chairs by one of her overstuffed bookshelves.

"I know that you already said that you didn't want to marry me, but I'd like you to reconsider my offer. Now, before you say anything, just hear me out." He sat forward in his chair, leaning closer to her and barreling forward before she could protest. "I think we should get engaged, on a trial basis. You don't have to actually marry me, but I want you to give me the chance to change your mind. Move in with me for one month, and if you decide to walk away at that time, then no hard feelings."

"Like a secret fake engagement?" She stifled a laugh and shot a glance to her shelf of family pictures. This wasn't a joke, and she should be taking this seriously. This was her life, her baby, her future she was dealing with.

"It won't be a secret, and it's only fake if that's what you decide. What I'm proposing is a trial engagement, and if you want out after you give it a month, then you are welcome to simply walk away. I won't try to pursue you if you decide it's not what you want after you've given it some time. I am interested in a real marriage, though. I didn't realize it in time to not behave like a complete ass to you, but I want to be a husband and a father, more than anything. After talking with your father, I got a pretty clear idea of how much this means to them, and I doubt anything less than marriage will be enough. If we get engaged, we're the only ones who have to know that it's on a trial basis. I want you to have time to decide if this is what you want, and I don't think your parents will wait around for you to make your choice. See, they'll be appeased while you're free to think it over."

"I thought that being seen with me was bad for your business." She raised her eyebrows. This wasn't the worst idea she'd ever heard, and considering how difficult her parents were making it, Richard's idea was looking good. They would prefer a quick marriage, but perhaps an engagement would stave off their anger for the time being.

"I think fathering your child and being nowhere to be found makes me look worse. This isn't just about how it looks for me, though." His tone was light, his smile easy. She suppressed a sigh, glad to finally have a solution she could live with. The thought of letting him take charge of the situation, having the decision made and her parents satisfied, was tempting.

"So you want to walk into my living room and tell my parents that we're engaged? And if we change our minds later, then what? I don't think they'll take kindly to that news."

"They won't, but surely even they wouldn't want you to marry someone you don't want to be with, right? I'm not going to change my mind." His eyes were intense, reminding Yvette of a sea during a storm. "I never thought I would marry again, but that was before this."

She cast her eyes down, flattered. "Oh? I've changed your mind somehow?"

"I didn't want to even consider it after my divorce. But that's when I thought that marriage could survive on love alone, and having my relationship disintegrate on the whim of my ex-wife's emotions was devastating. This time is different because there's a child involved, and it's not just two people following their feelings. There's more to it than emotion, there's a real family this time, and I think we can go the distance."

While she would have enjoyed a declaration of love or some semblance of emotion, she had to admit that she would eventually feel manipulated if he hadn't been so forthright. Her hormones were crying out for romance and bonding, but she knew that she couldn't realistically expect that from Richard, not just because they were suddenly tied together by the baby. Marrying him would make everything so much easier, even the trial engagement would help take the pressure off of her. It likely wouldn't be enough for long, though. Her parents wouldn't be satisfied until she was wed, and she knew that it didn't even matter to them that she and Richard weren't in love. He was right. Couples married for far less compelling reasons than bringing a baby into the world. At least this was honorable, and much more appealing than the thought of slogging her way through parenthood alone. If she were Mrs. Richard Morgan, she could hold her head up high, could go to sleep each night knowing that she had created a family for her child.

Getting married because of an unplanned pregnancy was never how she saw her future, had always assumed that true love and happiness would come. She couldn't escape her faith, wouldn't compromise her chance to have a traditional family, though. So they were doing things out of order, so what? There was no reason love and happiness together couldn't follow the marriage.

Despite herself, her heart swelled as she considered the possibilities, emotions or hormones working their magic when she looked into Richard's eyes. When they weren't at odds, he was so appealing, so charming. She would worry about love later, would hope for happiness in the meantime. The mess she found herself in now was too big to quibble over whether or not their marriage would be a love match, and the trial engagement meant that she didn't have to decide for now anyway.

She blinked against hot tears and swallowed against the lump forming in her throat. Damn hormones. "Yes. Okay. I'll do it."

A gorgeous smile spread across his face. "Yes? You mean I don't have to grovel or anything?"

She laughed and let him take her hand in his. "No groveling required. You're right. It's a good idea, and there's no harm in getting engaged and giving it a try."

"Now who's taking the romance out of it?" He teased. He pushed his hand in an interior jacket pocket and produced a small black velvet box. He slid off the chair and kneeled in front of her. He flipped the box open and plucked the ring out, took her left hand, and looked up at her. "Yvette Cruz, will you marry me?"

"You bought me a ring," she whispered, delighted despite herself, and struggled to remember why she'd ever said "no" in the first place. He slid the ring on her finger and she gasped. "It's stunning, Richard. Oh my gosh, it's beautiful." The ring was easily two carats—a sparkling, brilliant, princess cut diamond solitaire set on a heavy gold band. Staring into the exquisite facets, she could almost forget that this wasn't much more than a business arrangement.

"That's why you said 'no' last time, right? No ring?" He joked with her, his eyes dancing as he looked up at her. It would be so easy to pretend that this was real, and a part of her wanted to do just that.

She laughed and wiped a tear from her cheek. "Yep, that's why. I'm glad you got it right this time." She took a deep breath. "All right, now for the tough part. Are you ready to face my parents?"

He stood and pulled her up beside him. "Absolutely. Now that we've got an engagement to report, it's a piece of cake. If you had said no, I think I would've just camped out in here until your dad left. I couldn't face him again." He shuddered dramatically, causing her to giggle.

"He's not that bad," she said with a playful pat on his arm. Richard leveled her with an incredulous look. "Okay, he is that bad. Come on."

She led Richard out of her library and into her living room to face her stone-faced parents and deliver the happy news.

•••

"Rich! Long time no hear." Robert's voice boomed over the phone.

"Glad I caught you. I never know when you're going to be busy partying with rock stars or trashing hotel rooms."

The laugh on the other end of the line brought a huge grin to Richard's face. Robert was an incredibly successful record producer in New York, worked with huge musical acts, and he was all business, the consummate professional. He'd never trashed a hotel room in his life, but the raucous laughter reminded Richard of the fun they always had together.

"You know me. It's a crazy life." Robert still had a smile in his voice. "So what's up?"

"Something big happened, and I wanted to tell you first, but I saw Dad at work and ended up spilling it. I just couldn't wait."

"Well? Don't keep me in suspense."

Richard took a deep breath. "I'm engaged."

"No freaking way!"

"And I'm going to be a father."

"Are you serious? That's incredible. Congratulations, man. I didn't even think you were seeing anyone. Who's the lucky lady?"

Dad hadn't seemed too surprised that he was engaged, but then he had practically pushed Richard into it. That it was to Yvette was a bit of a shock, though. When he found out he was going to be a grandfather, he was so over the moon that he didn't care who Richard married or how it happened. "Her name's Yvette Cruz, and she works for that candy company that is negotiating with Dad about buying out our confections division."

"What? And you didn't go running in the opposite direction when you met her?"

"Well, yeah, that would've been logical. You'll have to meet her, though, and then you'll understand. She's smart and funny, gorgeous, and of course, pregnant with my child."

Robert laughed. "I can see why you'd marry this woman. What did Dad say? Is he cool with you marrying the enemy?"

"That's the thing. He's liked her all along. To him, selling off confections frees up resources for the divisions he really cares about. He and Yvette get along like two peas in a pod, and of course he loves the idea of being a grandfather, so he's over the moon."

"Me too, bro. I think I'll make a great uncle."

"Well, as long as you're happy." Richard teased.

"I can't wait to meet her, but I don't know when I'll be in town again. We'll have to figure something out."

"You can't come to the benefit?"

"I don't think that's going to work out. I'll check my schedule and pick a weekend or something soon. It's been too long."

"It has. Just let me know."

They ended the call, and Richard hummed to himself as he wandered around the house making room for Yvette's things. Now that he'd told his dad and brother, it was real. Their enthusiasm was further proof that this was the right move, and he couldn't wait to get started on their engagement.

•••

A few days later, Yvette sat cross-legged on her bed, smoothing her hand over the thick comforter, as she watched Richard tape a box closed. "Are you sure you don't want some help?"

He looked up at her with a sly grin on his face. "What are you saying? You don't enjoy the view?"

She laughed and tossed a tiny throw pillow at him. "I'm enjoying the view just fine. I just thought you might want some help packing my things." The truth was that she really did enjoy watching him from her vantage point. Richard looked positively edible in his soft black shorts and fitted grey t-shirt, the faintest hint of sweat popping up along his spine. Taut muscles moved beneath the bronzed skin of his forearms as he packed boxes and stacked them on top of one another. His toned, powerful legs begged for her touch, and her fingertips tingled at the thought of sliding her hands up his thighs. Those pregnancy hormones were working overtime again.

"I don't want you lifting a finger today. Just sit there and look beautiful." His sweet, genuine smile gave life to the butterflies fluttering in her stomach.

"Richard, I'm pregnant, not disabled." She allowed herself a moment to appreciate his compliment. She was wary of his new attitude towards her, waiting for him to put up his wall of resistance, but his charm hadn't slipped once since the day he proposed. He'd been open, friendly, and enthusiastic about the future, until she finally relented and started letting herself enjoy their developing relationship. Their easy chemistry was so genuine that she had almost decided to let herself give the engagement a real chance. Almost.

She'd promised herself to try to keep her wits about her, but it was growing more difficult the more time they spent together. Everything about him appealed to her lately, even more so since he had softened towards her, and everything he said was just right. It might be unwise to surrender to the relationship, but she was running out of reasons to stop herself. He hadn't given her any reason to mistrust him. There'd been no early declarations of love, no hint of anything less than genuine, and no sign of his earlier wariness.

"I know that, sweetheart. Let me do this for you. I want to." His voice was soft, and she warmed in reaction. The pet name, the sweetness—it was a lot to take in. "Save your energy for when we move your furniture."

"You mean *if* we move my furniture," she teased. Yvette wasn't ready to move out of her house completely. The only thing worse than calling off the engagement would be if she had to move everything she owned back home with her. Until she was sure, her house would be standing ready for her.

He stood and stretched, revealing a sliver of bronzed skin between the top of his shorts and the bottom of his shirt. "No, I mean *when*. I'm making it my mission to win you over within the month. By the time the trial period is over, you won't want an out." He walked over to the bed and leaned over her, warmth from his body surrounding her.

Her voice was shaky with desire and nerves when she spoke. "Oh, really?"

"Yes, really. The more I think about it, the more I like the idea of marrying you and building our family together. I'm happy to do whatever it takes to convince you as well." He put an arm on either side of her and got close enough so that his lips almost touched hers. "How am I doing so far?" He whispered against her lips.

She swallowed, unable to find her voice. She nodded and squeaked out, "So far so good." As a young girl, she had entertained plenty of fantasies of her future husband. He'd be someone strong, powerful, and brave. Once she fought cancer and learned that she didn't need a man to rescue her, she figured out that she'd rather have someone smart and kind, maybe handsome, but definitely loving. Richard was smart and handsome, and he was becoming kind and loving. Could he eventually become her ideal man? He certainly met all the qualifications. The only thing missing was the mutual love she knew she'd need in a marriage. Maybe that could even come in time. For now, she could enjoy their developing relationship knowing that her family was satisfied and she had time to figure out what she wanted.

He gave her a rakish grin and captured her lips with his own. His kiss was soft at first, as he smiled against her lips and murmured. "Now that's what I like to hear."

He ran his fingers through her hair, coaxing her lips open with his. Surrounded by his warm masculine scent, she breathed deeply and returned the kiss. With an arm snaked around her back, he slid her towards the headboard until she lay on her pillow and joined her on the bed. Her heart beat faster, head spinning, as he straddled her hips and lightly ran his fingers up her sides until he reached her face. Bending over her, he supported his weight on his elbows and buried his face against her neck. Shivers ran down her spine as his breath whispered across her skin. She felt her body respond to his touch, her hips arching to meet him without conscious thought.

Richard unbuttoned her blouse, slowly, as he kissed her. She thrust her fingers through his dark hair and wriggled beneath him. Gone was the man who had sneered when he saw her, the man who spent a night with her merely to rid himself of his desire for her. He was gentle now, caring and tender. He had changed. She ran her fingers through his hair, luxuriating in the soft dark locks as his kiss opened up feelings she was tired of suppressing.

Having the trial engagement's clear one month deadline in place made it so much easier to open up and enjoy everything their relationship had to offer. No more worries about giving up power or losing control of the situation, no winners or losers, just two people. Two people who enjoyed one another immensely.

Chapter Seven

The following Friday morning, Richard accompanied Yvette to her prenatal visit. They'd lived together a week, but nothing brought home the reality of the pregnancy like sitting in the obstetrician's waiting room. She was serene, flipping through a fashion magazine as they waited. Richard, on the other hand couldn't still his bouncing knee to save his life.

"Our appointment is at ten, right? What's the hold up?" He whispered.

She laid a hand on his knee. "Relax. He's not even fifteen minutes late yet. As long as he's here and not stuck at the hospital with a delivery, we'll go back any minute now."

"If you say so."

A nurse in pink scrubs poked her head through the doorway. "Ms. Cruz? We're ready for you."

"See? That wasn't too bad." She stood and he joined her, unsure for the first time since they'd arrived what he was supposed to do. "You can come back with me if you want."

Of course he wanted to. Feeling an odd mixture of excitement and fear, he followed Yvette and the nurse down a short hallway, past closed doors and bustling nurses. They stopped in a small lab area where the nurse checked her weight, temperature, and vital signs before directing her to the restroom for another test. He was led to an empty exam room to wait, and he dropped onto the generic office chair beside a plastic model of the human uterus, complete with baby. Yvette returned with the nurse and settled onto the paper-covered table to answer more basic questions, and within moments, they were alone in the tiny room.

"They really check everything, huh?" Richard shifted in the chair and clasped and unclasped his hands.

"Yes, and I think it gets more involved the further on in the pregnancy I get."

The doctor knocked and entered, greeting Yvette as he washed his hands in the tiny sink. Richard sat, feeling like an interloper, as the doctor and Yvette talked about the pregnancy. When she laid back on the exam table, the doctor invited Richard to listen as he positioned the Doppler wand over her abdomen.

"Will we see the baby? Can you tell if it's a boy or a girl?" Richard leaned over the table to see what was happening.

"Not today. I'm just checking for the heartbeat. We'll be able to determine the baby's sex around the twentieth week." The doctor moved the wand until it picked up a light sound. "There it is."

It was fast, maybe too fast, and strong. Richard grabbed Yvette's hand and squeezed as he looked into her eyes. "Oh my God, that's our baby."

"It's hard to believe." She smiled up at him, the moment stretching out between them.

He knew there was a baby, and he knew it was his. As much as Richard thought he'd come to terms with the fact, it wasn't real until he heard the heartbeat. There in the tiny exam room, strumming along like a little bird, was his son or daughter. And the woman who would make him a father.

"It's incredible." He managed to choke the words out, his throat thick as he let the enormity of the truth fall over him.

"A miracle." Her eyes shone in the room's fluorescent light, holding his future and everything he'd ever wanted.

"All right, Mrs. Cruz," the doctor began as he turned off the Doppler wand and she pulled her shirt back down. "Everything looks great, so we'll see you again in a couple of weeks."

"Thank you," Richard answered for them both, though he didn't look up from Yvette's face.

She sat up, using his arm to help her. "Thanks for coming with me."

"Of course. I wouldn't miss this for the world. Anything you need, anything I can do, just say the word."

"Right now all I need is lunch and maybe a warm bath. I have the rest of the afternoon off."

For a man used to handling every aspect of his life and career, watching the pregnancy unfold with nothing he could do to help was torture. "Then I also have the rest of the afternoon off. Let's get you something to eat."

•••

After a leisurely late lunch, they returned home to an empty house. Richard dropped his keys on the table in the foyer and followed Yvette into the living room, still elated from hearing his baby's heartbeat for the first time.

"Let's get you into a warm bath." His hand landed at the perfect spot between her shoulder blades, and he rubbed in small circles. "I'll make you some herbal tea and run the water while you get out of those shoes."

"That sounds like heaven."

He didn't know how she managed to spend the day in shoes like that, but he had to admit that she looked good doing it. With a pat on her butt, he gently pushed her towards the hallway. "I'll be there in a second."

Before going to the kitchen for her tea, he allowed himself a long look as she walked away. He was a lucky man, and he thanked God he was smart enough to realize it before he did something stupid. He'd proposed for almost purely selfish reasons, but the more time he spent with Yvette, the more he knew it was real. That steady, strong little heartbeat was the sweetest thing he'd ever heard, the best gift he'd ever been given. And it was all because of her, because she was willing to overlook his flaws while he got his head straight, because she was willing to extend grace when he didn't deserve it.

Careful not to spill the steaming mug of tea, he wandered down the hallway towards their bedroom. Her stilettos lay on the floor between the door and the bed, and instead of finding Yvette in her dressing room getting ready for her bath, she was curled up in a ball on the bed, still wearing the silky robe she must have changed into, already asleep. He set the cup down and, as carefully as he could, he eased the blankets back and tucked her into bed. She stirred, murmuring and pulling the pillow tighter under her head. The pregnancy was exhausting her, and she needed her rest so badly. Glad to have a chance to care for her again, he kissed her forehead and turned out the lights so she could sleep.

When he came back to bed that night, her deep, even breaths were the only sound in the dark room. As he slipped in beside her, she didn't fully wake, but curled herself against him. With her head tucked under his chin, her body perfectly matched against his, he wrapped his arms around her. Her lips brushed against his chest, sending the familiar attraction through him, but squeezing his heart as well. Things were different now, more real, more important. Knowing that Yvette was going to be the mother of his child and actually hearing that child's heartbeat were worlds apart. With a light touch, he ran his fingertips over her back, gliding across the silky fabric of her robe.

"You're here," she murmured against his chest.

"I'm here." She moved against him, her body gliding across his and giving rise to a hunger for her.

Any space between them was torture; he wanted every inch of her touching him and held her close, closer than he'd ever held her or anybody else. He wanted to tell her what she meant to him, to somehow express how full his heart was, but there were no words. How could he tell her that being with her was everything? That she'd given him the one thing he always wanted, the only thing he ever truly cared about? No words were adequate, and he couldn't push them past the lump in his throat if they were. Without a sound, Richard pushed her robe open and held her in his arms, desperate to hold her, unable to let her go.

•••

Yvette awoke late on Saturday morning, much later than usual. Since moving in with Richard, she'd quickly become accustomed to taking the time to care for herself, much more than before the pregnancy. She was nearing the third month, and found that few things interested her more than sleep lately. Well, except for sex, and that was becoming increasingly frustrating given the unsure nature of her feelings for both Richard and their relationship. He was all too happy to oblige her ill-advised, and increasingly frequent sexual advances, and after no more than a few days under the same roof, it had started to feel like a real relationship was developing between then. Yvette knew that it would be far wiser to keep her wits about her, to keep her emotions at bay, but it was so much easier and enjoyable to just give in. To finally fall in love for real.

With her stomach rumbling and her need to find him growing, she pulled herself out of bed, stepping over the silk robe she'd fallen asleep wearing. Realizing that she was naked except for a tiny pair of lace panties that could barely cover her growing midsection, she opened her closet door. She pulled on a pair of stretchy black yoga pants and swiftly yanked a soft pink t-shirt over her head. She caught a glimpse of herself in his mirror as she left the closet and smiled at her mussed hair and rosy cheeks. Life with Richard was turning her into a wanton woman, and she was happily going along for the ride.

She padded barefoot down the hallway towards the kitchen, peeking into his office and the other rooms on the way without seeing a trace of him. Bustling noises in the kitchen perked her interest and a slow smile spread across her face. She tiptoed around the corner, eager to see him.

"Good morning, dear." Mrs. King, the housekeeper, was behind the breakfast bar, drying dishes.

She had been looking forward to seeing Richard, but Mrs. King was a welcome sight. She was exactly as Yvette had imagined her when he mentioned that he had a full time housekeeper: short, round, and bustling. Her raven hair was streaked with silver and secured at the nape of her neck in a tidy bun, her charcoal grey uniform neatly pressed and free of stains, and she was always ready with an easy smile and a kind word. Her brisk, matter-of-fact manner made it easier for Yvette to accept being cared for by an employee.

The fact that Richard didn't find it strange to have someone cooking and cleaning for him, moving about his home with complete freedom, amazed her. She'd hired the occasional maid service when work was piling up and her house was a wreck, but never in a million years had she contemplated hiring full-time help. Not that she could afford it on her salary, even if it wasn't a ludicrous idea. Saffron kept her busy, some weeks working insane hours, but if Richard needed Mrs. King working every day to maintain his household, he must work even more. At least she hoped he employed her because of his crazy work schedule. That he might feel entitled to such pampering was simply too foreign to consider.

"Would you like some tea, dear?" Mrs. King held up the tea kettle in question. She had learned quickly that Mrs. King knew about the baby and wouldn't be offering coffee, no matter how much she craved the caffeine. The housekeeper was a sweet, motherly woman, but Yvette knew better than to argue with her.

"Sure, thank you." She settled onto a cushy barstool and watched as Mrs. King prepared her tea. "Have you seen Richard this morning?"

Mrs. King set a steaming mug of tea in front of Yvette and gave her a kind smile. "Mr. Morgan is at the gym, and then he is planning to go to the office for a couple of hours from there. He said he expects to be home for dinner but said that you are not to wait for him if he's running late."

"Do you know which gym?" He could be at his office's fitness center or the gym close to their neighborhood. It wouldn't hurt her to visit him, maybe share a workout. Between the move, work, and the pregnancy, she was lucky to stay awake through dinner and missed the energy a good workout could provide.

"Mr. Morgan didn't say for sure, but he left with racquetball equipment." Mrs. King dried a mug and smiled kindly at Yvette.

"Oh, I see." She hid her disappointment behind another sip of her tea and rested her elbows on the bar. "It's just as well. I should probably think about catching up on work myself. It'll be nice to have some peace and quiet." Work had been low on her list of priorities in light of everything else happening in her life lately, and Saturday or not, catching up might not be the worst idea. "Thank you for the tea."

She slid off the barstool and made her way back to the empty bedroom and into the en suite bathroom. She turned on the shower, and as the water warmed up, she brushed her teeth and considered herself in the ornate pewter-framed mirror. Her long dark hair was still mussed from both sleep and Richard.

She stepped into the shower and let the warm water wash over her, let her cares and concerns drift away for the moment. Spending the day catching up on work held little appeal when she let her mind drift to the new life she was enjoying here in Richard's home. Wouldn't it be nice to make it more hers? To put her own signature spin on it today? Great ideas always came to her in the shower, so a new plan for the day quickly took shape.

After drying off, pulling on jeans and a T-shirt, and applying a little makeup, Yvette made her way through the house to find Mrs. King. They had some shopping to do.

• • •

Richard let himself in the house and dropped his keys in their bowl on the table, and stopped. Festive salsa music drifted through the house, drawing him in towards the kitchen. Coming home to an empty, silent house like he used to seemed like a sad, distant memory now that Yvette was there, breathing life into the house and giving everything a spicy flavor. Getting out of his first marriage was such a relief—so important for his mental health—that he came to relish the silence. Now that it was gone, chased away by a Puerto Rican goddess, he never wanted to experience it again.

Rounding the corner, he caught a glimpse of Yvette as the music grew louder. She danced around the kitchen, singing softly to herself in Spanish as exotic aromas filled the air. Her hips swayed with the beat, hypnotic and enticing. His fingers twitched as he moved forward, itching to touch her. Her back was to him, and he took a moment to savor the uninterrupted moment, watching her in her element. She was a vision, the undulating curves, the sweet soft voice singing in a language he couldn't understand, the heavenly aromas bubbling up around her. How had he ever thought he could resist her? Why had he even tried?

She pulled an oversized silver spoon off the spoon rest and sang into it, throwing her head back and belting out the tune as she twisted in time with the music. As she turned, she noticed him standing there, and a slow smile spread across her face as she sashayed across the kitchen to meet him, hips still swiveling to the beat.

Wrapping her arms around his waist, she pulled him close, encouraging him to move along to the music with her. The song enveloped them, and they swayed together, slower and slower than the beat, until they were completely off the rhythm. She burst into melodic laughter and tipped her head up to accept a kiss.

"Welcome home. Hope you're hungry." She spoke softly, her lips moving against his before she danced back to the stovetop to tend to the food.

Richard leaned over her and looked into the pots bubbling on the stove. "This smells wonderful. I didn't know you cooked."

"Oh yes, all the women in my family cook. My sister and I learned from my mother and her sister, who learned from their mother and her sister."

"What is this?" A mixture of seasonings and chopped up bits simmered in the pot.

"That's my mother's *sofrito*. It's a seasoning sauce she makes in huge batches, and she always saves a couple of jars for me. I know how to make my own, but I've been so busy with work that I haven't cooked like I used to. I got the idea to make this dinner for you this morning, but then I realized that you don't have a big enough pot, so I went home and got mine and grabbed my spoon and the *sofrito* while I was there. Mrs. King and I did the grocery shopping and then I sent her home early. So we're alone." She wiggled her eyebrows suggestively, a playful smile on her face.

"You have a special spoon?" He wondered if the pregnancy hormones were making little things seem more important than usual.

"Of course I do. It's practically a rite of passage in my family to get your own big pot and spoon." She grinned and his heart skipped a beat.

"So what are we having?" He inhaled the aroma as she tossed chopped garlic, peppers, and pimientos into the mix.

"Ah, you're going to enjoy this." She waved the big spoon over the pot with *sofrito*. "I'm going to make *arroz con Habichuelas*, my special Puerto Rican rice and beans, *tostones*, crispy plaintains with salt and garlic, and *pasteles,* kind of like tamales. You're going to love it. I've got *tembleque* in the fridge for dessert." Her accent was coming out as she talked about the food, and his body was responding in all sorts of ways as he was drawn to the spicy, sultry sound.

"*Tembleque?* What's that?"

"It's a coconut custard dish, very sweet and refreshing. Delicious." She held her fingertips to her lips and made a kissing sound.

"If you keep talking like that, we won't make it to dessert." He grinned down at her and skimmed a palm over the curve of her hip.

"You don't want to miss it. Trust me." She tapped him with the spoon. "Go get cleaned up and I'll finish dinner."

•••

Thoroughly stuffed after gorging himself on the Puerto Rican dishes Yvette had prepared, Richard sat back in his chair and stretched. "That meal was absolute perfection. Mrs. King might have some competition."

"I think her job's probably safe for now. I can't eat like that every day, much less spend that much time cooking. I'd never be able to do much else."

He patted his stomach. "Yeah, I guess I'll need an extra hour at the gym to make up for that. It's was more than worth it, though. If nothing else, I wouldn't mind watching you cook again." After watching her sway to the music, he could think of a few ways to burn calories.

She raised her eyebrows and teased. "Oh? You prefer your women in the kitchen?"

"Only when they look like you." She continued to surprise him, to show her many different sides. Each time he learned something new about her was a revelation, yet another reason he was falling for her.

Her eyes danced playfully in the dining room's dim light. "My father used to tease my mother like that. She spent most of my childhood in the kitchen. It seemed like as soon as breakfast was over, she was getting lunch ready, and then dinner after that. Meals like this take so much time, between the planning and the shopping, not to mention the hours you spend actually cooking. She stopped making such huge meals every day when I got sick, since we spent so much time in treatment and I didn't have the appetite for it anyway."

"I'm sure that was tough on the whole family."

"You have no idea." She smiled sadly and pushed her chair back. "I'll go get the *tembleque*."

He watched her walk away, indulging himself in a long, lingering look at her hips as they rocked with each step. From behind, he could forget that she was pregnant and pretend that theirs was a typical courtship, not that he had any complaints about the view from the front. She complained about her weight gain, but as far as he was concerned, impending motherhood was agreeing with her. Her curves became more lush, everything about her glowed, as though she were in full bloom. With every moment they spent together, he grew more attracted to her. Already their home life was more normal and satisfying than he would have anticipated. After being certain that proposing to his pregnant rival would lead to at the very least an awkward transition, the easy banter they shared each day was a welcome surprise. They moved throughout their days in harmony, and their nights together were satisfying needs he didn't know he had.

Her hips swayed tantalizingly as she made her way back to the dining room holding the plates. "Come sit with me," he said as he patted his thigh.

She paused for the briefest moment before joining him. He pushed his chair back to make room as she set the dishes on the table and sat on his lap. Her legs were bare beneath the skirt of her wrap dress, and he couldn't resist sliding a hand up her thigh. She treated him to a throaty laugh, and he shifted beneath her as he hardened in response. That laugh was the one that pushed him over the edge their first night together, the one that turned his brain off and his body on.

She scooped a bite of the *tembleque* with a spoon and watched him through lowered lashes as she fed him. The cool coconut custard dessert melted in his mouth, and his eyes closed as he groaned in appreciation. "I'm never letting you go."

"I would have thought it would take more than good cooking to get a man like you." She teased, obviously pleased with his compliment.

"First, it's not just good, it's great cooking, and second, you're the complete package."

"You think so?" She took a bite of her dessert, her lips drawing his attention.

"Oh yeah. You're beautiful, smart, driven, *and* you cook like this?" He ticked off each quality with his fingers. "I couldn't ask for anything more."

With a soft kiss, she murmured as she fed him another bite. "I'm not going anywhere."

Richard pulled her closer and pressed his lips to hers, lost in the warmth of her silky skin, her fragrance surrounding him. He plunged his fingers into her hair and coaxed her lips open with his own, tasting the sweet cool dessert in her mouth. A tiny sound bubbled up in her throat and he hardened in response. Their tongues tangled, and he tasted cool coconut mixed with a desire that matched his own. Her spoon clattered to the floor as she wrapped her arms around his neck and pulled him closer to her. Everything fell away in the haze of wanting, needing, and for a moment there was nothing but Yvette. Her breath, her warmth, her curves.

With a deft hand, he pulled the belt of her wrap dress loose and smiled against her lips as she gasped. With his hands on her hips, he eased her around to face the table and settled her firmly on his lap. His fingers found the welcoming warmth at the apex of her thighs, and to his satisfaction, her legs parted at his touch. His free hand skimmed the silken skin of her hips, now rounder and softer, until he cupped her breast. She sucked in a sharp breath and shifted until her mouth could reach his for a searching, seeking kiss. Her hips rocked gently against him until his urge to press her against the table was too strong to ignore. Scooping her into his arms, he stood and answered her kiss with his own before taking her to the bedroom.

• • •

Hours after sating his hunger for Yvette, Richard sat at his desk catching up on work, when she appeared in the doorway. She wore a satin robe, demurely tied at the waist, and his mind drifted to their evening together. In the soft light of his desk lamp, she was like something out of a dream, tousled and wild, but sweet and welcoming.

"Hey, beautiful. Did I wake you?" He set his pen down and gave her his attention.

"No, I was just thinking about something and wanted to talk. I guess I need to talk to you." Her tone was light, but something alarmed him. That phrase was rarely followed by a simple matter.

Richard shifted in his chair. "Okay, what is it?"

"Things have been so nice between us that I hesitate to bring it up at all, but I want to get it out in the open. How are we going to handle our work problem?"

He sucked in a breath. It had to come up sooner or later, but he wasn't sure how to tell her that there would be no more negotiations now that they were engaged. True to his word, his father had given Richard control of the confections division after his engagement to Yvette. He'd let himself get caught up in the magic of the pregnancy and their developing feelings for one another, but it could all fall apart if she found out what he'd done. Taking a sip of water, he paused to consider how to answer.

"Hmm. Well, I think that leaving work at the office is the best way for us to handle it. My thoughts on your company buying out mine are not going to change, ever, but I don't want that to come between us anymore."

"It's kind of a big deal, though, don't you think? I mean, your company is everything to you, and it has been my job for months to try to take it. Do you really think we can just ignore it when we're at home?" He should have known that they couldn't ignore the elephant in the room.

"We could try. Would you rather talk about it?" This was dangerous territory. His father had suspended consideration of the acquisition, but apparently Yvette didn't know that. They'd come so far since she moved in, and things had changed so much between them. Revealing the deal he made would surely be the end of their relationship. His feelings for her went so far beyond the deal with his father that he couldn't risk telling her. She could never discover what he had done.

"It just seems like a black cloud hanging over us, you know? I've been thinking about it a lot lately and wonder if it wouldn't be better for us, and for the baby, if I asked to be reassigned."

He raised an eyebrow. "What does that mean for your job?"

She looked away. "It most likely means I'd be taken out of the running for the promotion I've been up for. Saffron is already investigating alternatives to our plans to buy your company, so I'm sure it's just a matter of time before they pull me off the account anyway."

A weight landed in his gut. She was willing to set aside her ambition for his sake? For their sake? Her failure to secure the buyout could set her back immeasurably, yet she wasn't going to ask for his help in making it happen. It was a huge professional sacrifice, and he was going to let her make it. There was no other way, not if he didn't want to lose her. And he didn't. He was dangerously close to falling in love with Yvette, and he couldn't bear her finding out what he'd done. "I truly don't deserve you."

Her eyes danced in the room's dim light. "Well, I don't know about that. I know it would be better for us as a family, but I'm not sure I can give it up. I may not have much of a choice, though, since my progress with your father has stalled anyway."

If he had taken another sip of his water, he would have choked. "Oh?"

"Yeah, I've had to pull back lately. He hasn't returned my calls or responded to any communication recently. We've been reevaluating our strategy since I can't continue to badger him. I shouldn't be talking to you about this, though, so that's all I'll say about that. If he wants to officially decline our offer, that's one thing, but the lack of communication makes me think that there's still a chance."

So she wasn't going to drop it. "I haven't changed my mind."

"That's fine," she sat up straighter. "But it's still not up to you."

It was in fact, up to him, but he couldn't tell her that. "True."

"So, until your father officially declines, our efforts stand. I think it would be better for us personally if I moved off the account, but it definitely wouldn't be better for my career. And honestly, it wouldn't be best for Morgan Confectioners, either."

He scoffed. "How's that?"

"Saffron doesn't want to buy out your confections division to hurt you or your company. We want to take what you've developed, put our marketing, branding, and research dollars behind it, and make it better than ever before. Morgan hasn't concentrated on confections in years, and it shows. You gained a little traction with the champagne lollipops, but I can't see how that's going to carry you much further. It just makes good business sense to take the momentum and build on it before it fizzles out."

"I'll take that under advisement. Thanks." His abrupt tone sounded confident to his ears, but it hid the growing disgust he felt for not only making the deal but keeping it from her.

God, he was a miserable excuse for a human being. It would've been easier if she'd continued to fight for the buyout rather than suggest the possibility of sacrificing her professional progress for the sake of their relationship. At least then he could be vindicated, could feel like he was simply fighting for his legacy. Her selfless act magnified what an underhanded liar he really was. He'd devote himself to becoming the husband and father she deserved, to give her the best life he could. It wouldn't make up for stalling her career growth, but it was the best he could do.

Chapter Eight

Yvette stepped into the enormous dressing room that Richard had emptied out for her, enjoying the feeling of her bare feet sinking into the plush carpet. She had lived with him for more than three weeks now, but the sheer elegance of his home continued to impress her. The dressing room was the size of an apartment bedroom and dwarfed even her own closets, large by anyone's standard. It was like the dressing rooms seen in movies, the kind most girls covet. A delicate crystal chandelier illuminated the room, beautiful ivory carpet covered the floor, an oversized full-length mirror dominated the room, and a chaise big enough to nap on sat beside a counter in the middle of the room. She could put her foldable items in the drawers contained within the counter and use the countertop for jewelry, accessories, and perfumes.

Tonight they were attending their first major event together since announcing their engagement. Pulling the dress she had chosen out of its garment bag, Yvette hung it on an empty rack, feeling fortunate that she had been able to find an elegant gown that covered her growing midsection modestly. She wasn't far enough along in the pregnancy for it to be obvious and feared that she simply looked chubby, despite Richard's steady enthusiasm and regular compliments for her changing body. As her body changed with the pregnancy, his demeanor changed. He'd surprised her with his excitement about the baby, his enthusiasm for the possibility of marriage, and how gentle he could be, how caring and doting. It was a far cry from the distant and argumentative man she'd met in Vegas.

Her month-long trial engagement was coming to an end, and she was surprised to find that she didn't have the slightest desire to leave. She wanted to believe that her hormones were working overtime to keep her bonding with Richard, but the truth was that he had changed, that their relationship had changed.

She didn't know if it was just the baby or something more, but she liked the new Richard. The more she got to know him, the more she wondered if she could fall in love with him, if maybe she already had. Their connection in the bedroom had become more intense, as though he were communicating his feelings for her when they reached for each other in the night. She found herself daydreaming about him when she was going through her day, craving his touch and dreaming of the future.

She pushed her freshly pedicured feet into a pair of the sparkly stilettos she had always favored and wondered how long she'd be able to walk gracefully in them. They still made her feel glamorous, sexy, like she was ready for anything, and knowing that in a few months she'd have to leave them on the shelf was just sad. After slipping on a pair of flawless diamond stud earrings she dabbed subtle perfume behind her ears and on her wrists. "You look amazing." Richard surprised her at the door. A frisson of electricity wound its way through Yvette's body as his silky voice caressed her. She wondered if she'd ever see him and not be immediately affected.

She whirled around to face him. "Thank you. You look pretty handsome yourself." She crossed the room to join him and allowed herself to drink in the vision of Richard in his tuxedo. Instead of becoming more accustomed to the attraction she felt for him, the pull towards him seemed to grow stronger the longer they were together, as though thousands of tiny threads knitted them together. She accepted his embrace and relaxed against his body as he buried his nose in her hair and inhaled deeply.

He cupped her face with his hands and planted a soft kiss on her lips, managing to infuse the chaste contact with longing and promise. "That dress is beautiful on you, but I think I'd like it more if it were crumpled in a heap on the floor."

She laughed. "You surprise me."

"Why? Because I'd rather ravish you than attend another boring benefit dinner?" He held a tendril of her hair between his fingers and gave her another kiss.

"No, that you'd use such a clichéd line. Now, get out of here, so I can get ready. We can't skip tonight. You're the guest of honor." When he turned on the charm, she was putty in his hands. If she let this go on one moment longer she'd have to reconstruct her hair and makeup, and they simply didn't have time for that.

Tonight, Richard's attention would be divided, with friends and family, dinner attendees, and business associates all vying for his time. He wouldn't be able to spend the entire night focused on her, but she knew that he would keep her close by his side. Before the evening ended, she'd be introduced to everyone important in his life and a hundred other people she'd likely forget. Since the engagement became public knowledge, it had seemed important to him that people know that they were together. Yvette didn't care what people outside of her family thought of her or her relationship with Richard, but she had to admit that it was nice to have him so willing to be open about it with the public.

•••

The hotel ballroom was awash with twinkling lights, the sounds of dozens of cultured voices chattering, and silverware clinking against china. Richard squeezed Yvette's hand as they entered the ballroom together and heads turned towards them. He kissed the top of her head and leaned down to whisper in her ear, almost close enough to taste her skin. "Ready to do this?"

She nodded and smiled up at him, stopping his heart for a second, and they made their way through the room. They wound through groups of people, occasionally stopping to chat, until they found their table towards the front of the room. Two of the eight chairs circling the table were occupied by Richard's college roommate and his wife. That left two mystery couples yet to arrive. One was likely reserved for his father and whichever woman managed to snag his attention enough to finagle a date. Yvette squeezed his hand, a gentle reminder that they were in this together. He pulled a chair out for her and she smoothed her dress under her as she sat. His breath caught in his throat when he looked down at her, grace and beauty wrapped in a stunning package.

He said hello to the guests at their table and took the seat next to her. He leaned over to whisper in her ear, noticing her subtle fragrance. "I'm pretty sure my father is seated at our table."

Yvette turned her head until her cheek brushed against his face. The brief contact sent a shot of longing through his body, and he wished the night would end soon so he could get her alone. She whispered, "You're not worried I'll try to talk shop all night, are you?"

"I'll just have to whisk you out of here if you do. I have ways to distract you." He laughed, but the truth was that he hadn't told her about the deal he and his father had struck. His father had agreed not to disclose their arrangement to Yvette, but things could become awkward if she decided to press the issue. All it would take to send everything bubbling over would be a casual remark about resuming talks, or a mention about missing opportunities if they didn't take her deal. Richard hoped that the conversation would remain social tonight, and he was determined to keep her focus on him and away from work.

He straightened up and introduced her to the couple seated at their table. "Yvette, this is my old friend, Brent Bixby. Brent, this is my fiancée, Yvette Cruz." Richard saw the flash of surprise on Brent's face as he leaned over to shake Yvette's hand. "This is Brent's wife, Penelope. Penelope, Yvette." He smiled at Brent's wife as she took Yvette's hand. Brent and Penelope had been married for years, and Richard had known them through their entire relationship. They were always urging him to find a wife and settle down despite his protests, so he knew that his engagement would come as a huge surprise.

"It's so nice to meet you Yvette." Penelope gave Yvette a bright smile and turned to Richard, wagging a finger between the two of them. "Now, when did this happen? We didn't even know you were dating anyone." Her eyes danced with excitement, as though he were joining some secret club. He knew the news that he had finally decided to settle down would thrill her.

"Well, I wasn't seeing anyone until I met Yvette. Let's see, we've been engaged about a month now, so things are really new for us still." Their one-month trial period was ending, and she'd shown no signs that she wasn't interested in moving things forward. It was amazing how fast the time had flown by. He smiled at Yvette before dropping a sweet kiss on her lips and turning back to Penelope. "You look lovely this evening, Pen. How are the boys?"

"Wonderful, growing like weeds, into everything, you know, being boys." Penelope's surprise at his engagement dissolved in her enthusiasm for chatting about her children. "Scott is in first grade now, and he's been taking piano lessons. It's the cutest thing. Ethan is in preschool, and he amazes me every day with the new things he picks up. Time flies, you know? It's crazy how fast they grow up."

"Wow. I can remember when those little guys were born." He smiled indulgently at Penelope.

"It is so nice to meet some of Richard's friends. How do you all know each other?" Yvette asked, leaning in to join the conversation.

"Rich and I met when we were freshmen in college back at the University of Pennsylvania, then we roomed together in business school at Wharton. And I work for Morgan Enterprises now. I guess I just couldn't stay away from this guy," Brent answered with a hearty laugh.

"He's being a little modest. Brent doesn't just work for Morgan Enterprises, he heads up our pet care division over in Reading. We'd be lost without him."

Penelope leaned in, propping her elbows on the table, barely concealing her curiosity. "Yvette, how did you and Richard meet?" Her eyes sparkled with interest as her lips curled back in an open smile.

"I've known about Richard for a long time, and we'd spoken on the phone," Yvette answered and Penelope nodded, "but I suppose the first time we actually met was at the Confectioners conference in Las Vegas."

Penelope looked intrigued. "Oh, so you work in candy too? You don't work at Morgan Confectioners, do you?"

Yvette started to answer, but Richard interrupted. "She works for Saffron Sweets."

Unsurprisingly, Brent looked confused. Richard had confided in him when talks began with Saffron about the transaction and the tension it had caused between him and his father. He laughed to diffuse the tension. "Our relationship has nothing to do with the business. I mean, look at her. I couldn't help but fall in love."

Yvette looked pleased by the compliment and gave him a sweet smile. It still surprised him how much things had changed between them. He planted a soft kiss on her lips, careful not to muss her lipstick.

The crowd stirred a bit, and the room's energy changed, became charged and electric somehow. He looked up to see his father approaching the table, stopping to kiss cheeks and shake hands as he wove his way through the crowd. Michael Morgan was a force of nature. He was brilliant in business, handsome, powerful, and most importantly, he still seemed accessible. Richard didn't see a woman accompanying him, but he was sure that he had brought a date, most likely someone half his age and completely inappropriate for him. Richard stood to greet him as he approached, then broke into a wide smile when he saw his younger brother, Robert, following close behind.

Sure enough, a gorgeous blonde caught up to them and grabbed onto his father's arm as he made his way through the room. Richard laughed to himself at the latest choice of companion. She looked like she would rather be anywhere but at a charity dinner for something as depressing as pediatric cancer. His father was a wizard at reading people and managing personalities when it came to business, but whenever a beautiful woman came into the picture he seemed to lose whatever sense he had.

They reached the table and enveloped Richard in a bear hug, giving him a few hearty pats on the back. Michael's date twirled a lock of gleaming platinum hair around perfectly manicured fingers as she scanned the room, looking bored.

"Robert, I can't believe you made it. It's good to see you, man, really good. What an awesome surprise." Richard couldn't stop smiling. It had been months since he'd seen his younger brother, and he didn't think he was going to make the trip from New York to join them at the benefit.

"I couldn't miss your big night. Besides, I wasn't convinced you were really engaged, man. I had to see it for myself, I guess." Robert clapped him on the shoulder. "I mean, if you're getting married, she's got to be something special. I had to get down here to meet the woman good enough to get you to take the plunge again."

"Son, it's always great to see you, but your lovely fiancée is positively breathtaking. Yvette, it's so nice to see you, dear." His father took Yvette's hand and kissed her fingertips when she stood to greet him. "We're practically family now. Give an old man a hug." He pulled her into an embrace that seemed to rankle his date, then stepped back and held Yvette at arms' length, giving her an appraising gaze. "How have you been feeling? You look absolutely radiant."

Yvette was clearly pleased by his compliment. "I've been a little tired, but I'm fine. I'm feeling good, and the baby's healthy. Everything's going well."

His father beamed at her, his chest puffed with pride and his eyes sparkling with affection. Richard couldn't remember the last time he had seen his father look so genuinely happy. Impending grandfather-hood agreed with him. He held her hands in his, grinning like a kid on Christmas until his gaze flitted over her left ring finger. His smile faltered for a second before he recovered it, and he stepped back from Yvette. "Well my dear, you look beautiful, just stunning."

Robert gave Richard a discreet thumbs-up sign before greeting Yvette. "I'm Robert, Richard's younger and much more handsome brother." She laughed and held out her hand to him, but he pulled her into a hug. "It'll be nice to have a woman in the family again. There's too much testosterone floating around the Morgan clan with just us three guys."

"I'm thrilled to be joining the family." She beamed at him, clearly in her element. She was his perfect match, and he could have gone the rest of his life without realizing it. Her traditional upbringing and closely held values were more in line with Richard's than he would have guessed. Months ago, he would have pegged her as the worst thing that could've happened to him. Now, she was the answer to dreams he didn't think he'd had.

His father leaned over to Richard and spoke softly, so no one could overhear. "That's not your mother's ring."

Richard stiffened. The ring he bought for Yvette was beautiful, a sparkling tribute to his developing feelings for her, but true, it wasn't his mother's ring. When Richard was eighteen, his father had given him his mother's wedding ring to give to his own bride someday. Chelsea had deemed it too modest for her taste, which should have alerted Richard to impending trouble, but didn't at the time. After the demise of his first marriage, Richard was so determined that he would never marry again that he'd locked it away in his safe deposit box. The ring represented everything that he would never have in this life: pure love, uncompromising commitment, untethered passion for another person. It was his one enduring link to his mother, and he never considered giving it to anyone else, no matter how greedy it seemed. He wanted it to keep her memory close to his heart, perhaps selfishly, and he would never pass it along to his own bride.

He glanced at her, and saw with relief that she was chatting with Penelope and didn't overhear the conversation. Surely she'd understand the significance of the ring sitting in the safe deposit box and would be hurt that it wasn't the one sitting on her finger. He knew that she wouldn't ask for it, but their developing relationship was so tenuous that he didn't want to take any chances.

Richard took his father's arm and moved him a few feet away from the table. "Our engagement was a bit rushed, due to the circumstances. My assistant helped me get Yvette's ring on short notice."

His brow furrowed. "You still have your mother's ring, right?"

"Of course I do. It's in my safe deposit box." Richard hoped his tone would end the conversation. Yvette wasn't stupid, and she wasn't unobservant. She was a proud woman, so surely she wouldn't ask him about the ring if she overheard, but he knew that it could hurt her.

"So, why not go get it?"

Richard shot a quick glance towards the table and noted with relief that Yvette was laughing at something Robert had said. He lowered his voice and leaned close, hoping his father would get the hint that he didn't want to talk about the ring. "Because I already gave her a ring."

"What, did you lose the receipt or something? I think your mom would've wanted her daughter-in-law to wear her wedding ring."

"I know. It's important, but it happened so fast. I just bought a ring and proposed. I didn't think about it at the time."

"Okay, I just think it's strange."

"I'll take care of it. Please don't mention it to Yvette until I do." Richard realized he was speaking through gritted teeth and took half a step back, deliberately relaxing.

"Whatever you say." His father clapped him on the shoulder and walked towards his seat, belatedly greeting the rest of the guests at the table. He introduced his date to everyone, and Richard was treated to a tepid smile and a limp handshake from her before she took her seat.

He breathed a sigh of relief. Surely his father would have his hands full entertaining his date and would drop the issue of the ring for the night. Penelope engaged Yvette in conversation, and Richard took the opportunity to mentally review his speech. He was looking forward to speaking to the crowd tonight. Unlike many people, he enjoyed public speaking and found that it was a great opportunity to influence giving when he spoke for causes that he believed in.

Yvette's hand found his thigh under the table and gave him a light squeeze. His focus flew from his impending speech to the warmth of her skin on his leg. What was it about her that got to him? It was a lot to wrap his mind around, but she had a way of calming him, of centering him, without even trying.

Suddenly, he became aware that all eyes were on him and realized that his name had been called. It was time to make his way to the front of the room and address the crowd. His fingers found the notes for tonight's speech in his pocket, and he stood, ready to project confidence and optimism. He cleared his mind and regained his focus as he reached the podium and moved the microphone up to his face to address the room.

• • •

When Richard addressed the crowd, you could have heard a pin drop. Yvette found herself transfixed as he talked about pediatric cancer, the toll on the families, the strain on businesses when employee productivity suffered. She wouldn't be surprised if the foundation reached their yearly donation goals in one evening after his impassioned speech. Yvette watched the faces in the crowd and everyone was riveted, hanging on Richard's every word.

She watched as he made his way through the crowded room, stopping to talk with donors, greeting acquaintances. He commanded respect but his charming, easy manner made him accessible. She watched him, mesmerized, as he interacted with the beautiful crowd. He was clearly in his element.

With a frisson of anticipation, she locked eyes with him as he made his way back to the table. Dozens of women lined his path back to her, but his eyes never left hers. The rest of the room fell away, faces blurred and voices faded away to a faint background buzz. He was fascinating, riveting. A force of nature. They walked back to the table arm in arm, and Michael rose to greet them, but wobbled a bit on his feet.

"Beautiful speech, son. Well done." He pushed the last word out, a bit breathless, and Yvette noticed how pale he looked. A faint shiver of fear shot through her and she took Michael's hand, finding it clammy. "Are you okay?"

Michael looked pale, and beads of sweat popped up along his forehead, but he nodded. "I think so. I'm fine. Just a little queasy."

Robert leaned over. "Dad? What's wrong?"

"Let's get you some water. I'm sure he's fine." Richard guided his father to his seat and put a hand on his shoulder as he sat down. Lowering his voice, he asked, "sure you're okay?"

Michael gulped down water until his glass was empty and nodded. Richard sat beside her and watched his father, concern etched on his features. Her hand found his under the table. Their fingers interlaced and she squeezed. She leaned over and whispered, her lips brushing his ear. "Should I find a doctor?"

Richard turned his head so that his cheek brushed her lips, his voice low. "Let's get him another glass of water and see." He raised his hand to signal for the waiter.

Suddenly, Michael slumped over in his chair, and his date caught him before he fell to the floor. When he clutched his chest, his date stood, wild-eyed, and searched the room for help. Richard was halfway to the microphone on stage before Yvette could pull her phone out of her clutch. She was dialing 911 when he called out for a doctor in attendance. His rich baritone was laced with panic, but he scanned the crowd with authority until a physician was located.

The doctor rushed to Michael's side and began assessing him. He checked Michael's pulse and turned to the guests at the table. "Does anybody have aspirin?"

The guests around the table shook their heads, and Penelope rummaged through her evening bag until she produced a small foil packet and passed it to him. The physician checked Michael's breathing, and helped him swallow the aspirin. He turned to Yvette. "Are you on the line with 911?"

She nodded and held up her index finger. She spoke into the phone, careful to keep her voice calm as she told the operator what had happened. "He is conscious and breathing. We have a doctor with him." She listened, and responded. "Thank you." She held the phone to her chest and addressed the physician. "Paramedics are en route." She handed the phone to Richard. "Here. Can you answer some questions about your dad?"

He took her phone and stepped away from the crowd around his father so he could speak with the dispatcher. With his head bent, he ran his fingers through his hair and puffed out a strong breath. Michael's date fled in panic, and Penelope and Brent worked to keep onlookers away from Michael while Robert knelt by his side, eyes wide with panic. The physician continued to monitor Michael and tried to keep him comfortable while Robert answered whatever questions he could. Eventually, a group of paramedics arrived, and the crowd parted as they made their way towards Michael.

Richard's father was loaded into an ambulance, and Richard and Yvette followed them to the hospital in a chauffeured town car. Tense silence stretched between them, the car's air conditioner and the hum of the road the only sounds. She watched him in profile, his strong jaw clenched and his eyes narrowed intensely as though he could will the traffic to move faster. The town car sped along behind the ambulance in the wake of the siren and flashing lights, and she struggled with whether to leave Richard to his thoughts or break the silence. Maybe he was the kind of person who remained calm in an emergency and allowed the emotions to come later. Surely he wasn't as unaffected and in control as he appeared.

"It's going to be okay. He'll pull through this." She laid a hand on his thigh and squeezed softly.

He covered her hand in his and turned to face her. "God, I hope so." His vulnerability finally cracked the surface of his confident calm, and her heart broke for him. Losing his mother likely made him fear the worst. "I tried to keep it together in there, to not panic when I wanted to, but it was so hard. You'd think by now I would recognize that Robert's not a little kid anymore. He doesn't need me to protect him from anything."

"I'm sure he's glad you've got his back." She leaned over and kissed his cheek.

He took her hands in his and looked her in the eye. "Thank you. I couldn't go through this without you."

She looked down at their intertwined hands. Her heart swelled with emotion, but the backseat of the car heading towards the emergency room wasn't the place to take the leap and admit to him that her feelings had grown. Now Richard needed her to be strong and supportive, a shoulder to lean on during the uncertainty of the next couple of hours. Her feelings would have to wait.

•••

Richard shifted in the waiting room's hard plastic chair and checked his watch. His father had been alive and conscious when they arrived in the emergency room, so he knew that things could be much worse. Still, the waiting seemed interminable. A pundit gesticulated wildly and shouted on the television mounted on the wall. He shook his head. So many things were meaningless in the face of such a potential loss. Michael Morgan was healthy, a hale and hearty man, and Richard wasn't ready to lose his only remaining parent. They had grown closer than ever in the years since his mother's untimely death. Between working so closely together and their shared loss, they had developed a fierce bond. Losing him would be like losing part of himself. Thank God he had Yvette by his side. Without her calming presence, he would be a nervous wreck.

He couldn't pinpoint the moment when he started seeing her in a different way, but his feelings for Yvette had turned around completely since the day they met. She had managed to change his mind without really trying. Just being around her lit him on fire, igniting all his senses, but it had grown into more than that. When he looked into her eyes, he saw his future, and it felt right. He saw his home, his family, where he belonged. It was all there, reflected in her eyes.

When Chelsea left, he was certain that he'd never fall in love again, that he wouldn't want to trust another woman, to let anyone into his heart. He promised himself that he would be fine living his life without love, that he didn't need it. But he didn't realize that he had no idea what love was. What he'd had with Chelsea was nothing, no more than a farce. Yvette was his everything, and it had happened right under his nose.

He looked up to see her return from getting coffee for them and watched her walk across the waiting room. As always, she stood out like a jewel in a bed of sand. Tonight she wore his jacket over her sophisticated couture gown but it didn't hide her incomparable beauty. Seeing her in such a drab, mundane setting highlighted everything that was right about her. She handed him a cup of coffee and their fingers touched. Then he knew. He was falling in love with Yvette Cruz—if he hadn't already.

She sat beside him and blew on her coffee. "Mine is decaf, of course," she said with a smile. "Yours is regular. It could be a late night."

"Thank you." He watched her sit back and realized that she must be exhausted. The pregnancy made everything harder for her, and tonight had been an emotional juggernaut. Yet she still took care of him and saw to his needs while he focused on his father. He angled his body so that he was facing her. "You must be exhausted."

"I'm glad to be here. I wouldn't leave you here to go through this alone." She shrugged, clearly not picking up on the depth of his emotions.

"I mean it. Being with you has made this bearable." He wanted to say more, to somehow express his growing feelings, but an emergency room waiting area wasn't the place.

Robert rushed in, out of breath, and dropped into the chair beside him. "I thought I was never going to find a parking space. Have you heard anything yet?"

"No, not yet. Dad's being treated right now."

"Robert, can I run and get you a coffee?" Yvette leaned over Richard, letting her hand rest on his thigh.

"Mr. Morgan?" A man wearing blue scrubs approached them before Robert could respond.

Richard stood, his heart in his throat, and Robert rose beside him. The moments it took the doctor to reach them from across the room were the longest of his life. Time stretched out interminably as he held his breath, desperate for news of his father's condition but terrified of what he may hear. With his younger brother at his side, the enormity of the situation hit him. They could lose another parent tonight, and he was so unprepared. He swallowed and took a deep breath. "I'm Richard Morgan. This is my brother, Robert."

The doctor stood in front of them and scraped his hand over his chin, addressing both of them. "I'm Dr. Summers. Your father is stable. It appears that he had a minor heart attack, and now he's resting. We'll want to run more tests to determine the extent of damage, and he'll need to be admitted, but for now it looks like he's out of the woods. You can see him if you like." He looked at Yvette, still seated. "One at a time, please."

"Of course. Go ahead, and take your time. I'll be fine waiting out here." She touched his hand and sat back in her chair, settling in so he could visit his father.

Robert touched his arm. "You go ahead. I'll sit with Yvette."

· · ·

He followed the doctor through the waiting room to his father's curtained-off bed. Michael Morgan lay amongst the tubes and wires, under the buzzing fluorescent lights, looking weak and old. His father had always been so healthy and vibrant, often mistaken for a much younger man. Seeing him made vulnerable, look-ing like a sick person in the oversized generic hospital robe, took Richard's breath away. Hot tears prickled behind his eyes, threat-ening to fall, when his father spoke.

"Don't count me out just yet." His raspy voice was soft but held a hint of his normal cheer. He smiled, tired and weak, up at him. "The doctor said it was a mild heart attack. Felt pretty major to me." He laughed at his own joke and pressed a hand to his chest. "It knocked me right on my ass."

Richard walked to his side and took his hand. "You gave everyone a scare, old man."

"Couldn't let you hog the spotlight." He said with a weak laugh before closing his eyes.

Richard filled a cup of water for his father and pulled a chair close to the bed. He laid a hand over his father's and watched his face.

His eyes fluttered open again, and he fixed his gaze on Richard. "Listen, I'm going to make some changes. I can't keep up this pace if I'm going to recover. I'd rather be around to play with my grandchild than risk another heart attack. If you're ready, I'll turn everything over to you."

"You don't think that's a bit hasty?" He wanted Morgan Enterprises, but he always thought it would come later. He was prepared to wait, to help his father during his recovery and then step aside when he was back up to speed. Taking over the company would mean that Richard acknowledged his father's new fragility, something with which he was not at all comfortable.

"I've got to focus on my recovery right now. When I'm well again, I can come back and advise you. If you think about it, this way the transition will be much easier. Won't it be nice for you to have me available to help out while you're settling into the position? If you wait until I'm gone, you'll be all on your own."

"I suppose so. I just don't want you making any rash decisions. There's no reason to think that you won't be back, better than ever, in no time."

"Sure, son. You can count on it. I have every intention of making a full and record-breaking recovery. Little scares like this can really make a man think, though. I don't want to run myself into the ground heading up Morgan Enterprises when I have a young buck like you just chomping at the bit to take over." His eyelids looked heavy, but he smiled at Richard.

"It's never been like that." Richard's voice was soft, and he swallowed past the lump that formed in his throat.

"I know. I'm only teasing you. We can work out the details later, but I am sure about this. I'll stay involved, but I want you to step up and take the wheel. Think about it. This way you don't even have to wait until you're married."

"Would you still consider this if I hadn't gotten engaged to Yvette?"

"Yes. This has nothing to do with our agreement and everything to do with my health going forward. You can consider the deal called off if you like. If you don't want to marry her, don't. Though I've seen the way you look at each other, and I think you'd be making a big mistake if you let her get away."

"Dad, no, that's not what I meant." He realized that his father likely thought he was cutthroat enough to propose to Yvette to gain control of the company. In light of how dramatically his feelings for her had developed, Richard felt sick over the thought of using her, for ever having considered it for a moment. It was a blessing that he'd never considered sharing the offer details with her and asking her to make a deal.

"It's fine. I shouldn't have pushed you into marriage like that. I wanted it so badly for you that I used the company to get my way."

"That's not why I proposed to Yvette," he hedged. If he were honest with himself, he had to admit that he had thought about the company when proposing to her. Thankfully he had fallen in love with the woman who was to be his wife before marrying her under false pretenses. Faced with the reminder of life's fragility and the now-firm knowledge that he loved Yvette, Richard desperately wanted to make the relationship work. She would never have considered their engagement without the one-month trial period he proposed, but now he wished they had never made such an agreement. He was ready to move forward with the marriage and begin their future together. As husband and wife, as a family.

"I know that the pregnancy forced your hand, but would you have done it if I hadn't made the offer? I mean, you didn't even give her your mother's ring, so I didn't think it was genuine. I figured this was about the offer—your honor maybe—but not for love."

The question sliced through him with its honesty.

He raked a hand through his hair. Richard hated to admit to himself that he had proposed marriage in order to further his career goals, but it was at least partly true. Saying it out loud would likely sound as despicable as he felt. "I don't know. It's more complicated than that, but there's a chance I wouldn't have. Things are different now, but of course I have to admit that your offer influenced me." He answered softly and hung his head.

"Don't be too hard on yourself. It was selfish of me to manipulate you like that. If your feelings for Yvette are real, I don't see any reason you can't put this business behind you and move ahead. She doesn't ever have to know."

"I guess you're right. At this point, since the offer's no longer an issue, it doesn't hurt to keep it from her. I think telling her would do more harm than good."

"Absolutely. I'll leave it up to you to decide how to handle this mess with Saffron Sweets from now on. You're going to have to figure out a way to tell Yvette that the decision is yours, though. I think I'm done dodging her calls and refusing to meet with her. I'm going to get to know her as my future daughter-in-law now and leave the tough stuff up to you." He laughed and smoothed the blankets around him.

"Fair enough," said Richard. "I'll let Robert come in while I check on Yvette and see how long it'll be before they move you upstairs to your room."

• • •

He returned to the waiting room, where Robert sat alone on the plastic chairs, checking messages on his phone.

He looked up as Richard approached, worry etched on his face. "How's Dad?"

"Stable. He'll be admitted and they're going to keep him at least overnight, but I think he's going to be okay. He was tired, but he felt well enough to crack jokes, so that's got to be a good sign. Where's Yvette?" He looked around the sparsely populated waiting room.

"She left. Something about work or something. I thought she told you when she went back there. Maybe a nurse stopped her?"

"Hmm. Maybe. They said one visitor at a time, but I'm surprised she didn't at least touch base with me before taking off. Oh well, I'm sure we'll catch up soon. You can go back and see Dad if you want. I'll wait here in case they need someone to fill out his paperwork or anything."

Richard dropped onto the seat and turned his phone on, only to find that while several dozen texts and voicemails had come in since their arrival, none were from Yvette explaining why she left in such a hurry. Perhaps he didn't know her as well as he thought he did, or perhaps she didn't care for him as much as he hoped. Was it possible that the growing feelings were one-sided?

Nothing at work should be more important than her future father-in-law and fiancé at a time like this—nothing. He'd let his developing feelings cloud his judgment, clearly. Leaving him alone in the hospital was something Chelsea would have done, then acted surprised when he called her out on her selfishness.

Who would've thought Yvette would do the same? He'd let himself believe that they could be a family, that he could finally have everything he wanted. They apparently had different ideas about what was important. At the first sign that Michael Morgan wouldn't be available for her to negotiate with any longer, she'd disappeared, maybe to reassess her strategy.

He dialed her number and slumped as her voicemail engaged on the first ring. "Yvette, it's me. Give me a call when you get this and let me know what's going on. I'm worried about you since you left in such a hurry without saying goodbye. Call me."

With a heavy sigh, he tucked the phone back in his pocket and looked around at the dismal waiting room, taking in the worried people in the chairs around him, the old magazines, the bored workers sitting at the front desk. He'd give Yvette the benefit of the doubt, give her a chance to explain, but for the life of him he couldn't think of anything that should pull her away from the emergency room without a backwards glance.

Chapter Nine

Yvette hadn't returned his calls or texts, hadn't come home, and was apparently screening her calls at work. After four days without contact, it was time to admit that she was gone. But why? Had things become too real for her? Had he somehow scared her off? If it weren't for the burning, persistent pain in his heart and the hollow emptiness that plagued his waking hours, he could convince himself that nothing had ever happened between them. She had swiftly and completely removed herself from his life; something he never would have guessed would be so painful.

Between visiting his father in the hospital and keeping in touch with Robert, he distracted himself with work, as he did when confronted with any other difficulty. He went in to the office early, stayed late, avoiding home until the latest hours of the evening, often returning with time for nothing more than falling into bed. Alone.

With Yvette apparently out of the picture and no further obstacles to the future of the company, he threw himself into projects that would push Morgan Enterprises to its highest level of achievements. After wanting control of the company so badly he could taste it, actually having it in his hands was a bitter victory. He took meetings, reviewed proposals, brainstormed with department heads, all to further the brand. When he was finished, every division of Morgan Enterprises would be the most profitable, most innovative leader each of their industries.

At home, alone, he sat in the dim light of the living room. Silence surrounded him as he focused on the rivulets of amber liquid trailing down the inside of his glass. Yvette's discarded engagement ring sat on the table beside him, the facets catching light from the lamp. Everything else of hers was gone, completely erased from his home. She'd left the ring behind to send a message, but without knowing what happened, the meaning was lost on him. He wracked his brain trying to remember the last conversation they'd had, anything that could have caused her to turn tail and run. Misery settled into his bones, heavy, holding him down and keeping him from sitting up enough to even reach the glass to take another drink.

The front door opened and softly clicked closed and footsteps echoed down the hall coming closer, but Richard didn't turn around at his brother's greeting. Instead, he let his head fall against the back of the couch and let out a long, slow breath.

"Come on in." With colossal effort, he waved a hand towards the stocked bar. "Grab yourself a drink."

Robert smirked and shook his head as he poured himself a drink. "Don't you think you're being a little melodramatic?"

Richard groaned, sitting up enough to reach his drink. "You were there, man. The love of my life walked out on me, and she's not coming back. She won't even take my calls."

"The love of your life? You've known her for what? A couple months?"

"A lot can happen in a few months." Richard finished his drink, perversely enjoying the burning sensation the scotch trailed down his throat. He deserved it, and the burn was better than the nothingness he'd been living with since Yvette walked out. "I don't know what I'm going to do."

Robert crossed the room and dropped onto a wingback chair, took a sip of his drink, and fixed Richard with a more sympathetic look. "Did you really want to get married again?"

"Yes. I wasn't sure at first, I mean, you know I thought I was done with marriage, but things changed. Once I found out about the baby, something clicked, and after she moved in, everything fell into place."

"I just think you might be romanticizing things a bit. I mean, you were dead set against marriage, and then you changed your mind just like that?" Robert snapped his fingers. "When you told me you were engaged, I couldn't believe it. Once I heard about the deal Dad offered you, it made much more sense though."

"I wasn't going to take him up on the offer. I mean, seriously. I wanted the company, still do, but I wasn't going to do it that way. It seemed crazy. This thing with Yvette just happened, with the baby, and her super conservative parents, and the next thing I knew, we were engaged."

"You weren't thinking of the deal when you proposed?" Robert raised an eyebrow.

Richard stared into his glass for a moment, disappointed that the first assumption was that he used a personal situation to strengthen his professional position. He couldn't blame him, though, since it was the sad truth. "Of course I'd be lying if I said I never thought about the deal, but honestly that wasn't my main motivator. Well—at first, I guess I *was* thinking about the deal, and maybe my reputation, you know? But once I spoke with her parents, I felt like it would be good for both of us if we at least got engaged."

"What do her parents have to do with it?" Robert took a sip of his drink.

"She comes from a strict, conservative Catholic family, and her parents still have a lot of influence over her. Apparently in her family, as long as she's a single woman, her father considers her under his protection. I really expected her to stand up to him, but they have a lot of influence over her."

"Man, I wouldn't have guessed she was that conservative. I mean, just from the little time I spent with her, she didn't seem like the type."

"Her dad sacrificed a lot for her when she was growing up, and she hated the idea of letting him down. She probably would've said no to me if it wasn't for her parents." He sipped his drink. "I thought she was completely focused on her career, actually kind of ruthless and always looking out for herself, but she was going to keep the baby regardless of what I did. Never even considered any alternatives. Turns out she really wants to be a mother and have a family of her own."

"Rich, that sounds a lot like someone I know." Robert offered the observation gently, his meaning clear.

Richard paused for a beat. "You're right. I didn't realize it before, but I think that's why we've clashed so much, and why I'm so drawn to her." He gulped. "I'm in love with her."

He didn't qualify it this time with a "maybe" or an "I think." He knew it was true and it felt good to say it out loud.

"So now you want to make this a real engagement? A real marriage?" Robert joked, laughing.

His brother's attempt to lighten the mood fell flat. "Hey, I think I could be a good husband. I certainly tried. "

"Except for the part where you got engaged under false pretenses and kept a huge secret from your intended." Robert's sarcasm was obvious. "Other than that, I'm sure you were a really good partner."

Richard set his glass on a table and stood, getting angry. "Yeah, sure, Dad offered that deal, but the thing with Yvette just happened! It was completely separate from Dad's offer. It all went down so fast, and everything fell into place. I wasn't trying to trick her or use her to keep the company. It just … happened like that." It sounded incriminating—or at least awfully convenient—even to himself.

Robert waved a hand dismissively. "I'm just giving you a hard time. And hey, Dad told me he offered you the company—no strings attached. I think he was trying to give me one more chance to claim my birthright and join you two." He shook his head.

"Couldn't pay me enough. Oh, and don't worry about Yvette. She never has to know."

He fell back onto the couch. "It doesn't matter. She's not talking to me anyway, and I don't even know why. I really thought things were progressing with us, that my past, Chelsea, none of that mattered. I thought she would be different."

"She's not different?" He sounded skeptical.

"Maybe I wanted things to be different with her, wanted them to work out. I don't know, but we met because she wanted to negotiate a buyout. I don't know that she ever stopped wanting that. I'm afraid that once she figured it would be impossible, you know, with Dad out of the picture, she didn't have use for me."

The amusement disappeared from Robert's face, and he leaned forward on his knees. "Seriously? That'd be pretty cold, but you know her best. So you think *she* was using *you* to get the deal?"

Richard scraped a hand across his face and looked towards the ceiling. "I don't know. I guess she's trying to make a clean break or something, but we can't go on like this forever. We have to talk some time, you know, for the baby's sake."

"True. If nothing else, you'll get your chance to see her when the baby is born. I hope you get this settled before then, though, or you're in for a long wait."

"There's no way I'm waiting that long. If she wants to end things with me, that's her choice, but I won't let her play me for a fool. This ends tomorrow. One way or another, we're going to talk." Even if she did leave to reassess her business strategy, he was in love with Yvette and wanted her back. They'd find a way to make it work. There was simply no other option.

•••

Yvette refused to take his calls, so Richard took a page out of her playbook, and hopped in his car to confront the situation head on. Surely she would give him a moment to plead his case when he showed up at her office door. She'd done the same thing to him. With any luck, she'd appreciate the irony and his willingness to take a chance. He left his car in the parking garage at Saffron Sweets, and jingled his car keys in his pocket as he rushed to the elevator. His footsteps echoed in the concrete structure, reminding him how alone he was.

The journey from the parking garage to Yvette's office seemed interminable, until he finally reached the correct floor and approached her office. Her assistant sat at a desk outside her door, apparently prepared to keep her safe from unwanted visitors, such as the father of her child. The young man smiled up at Richard pleasantly and asked how he could help.

Richard looked down at the name plate sitting at the front of the desk and gave him his most disarming smile. "Good afternoon, Tate. Richard Morgan to see Ms. Cruz."

Tate turned to his computer screen, brow furrowed. "Mr. Morgan, I don't have an appointment for you, and Ms. Cruz is not receiving visitors right now. May I tell her you stopped by?"

He gave the assistant a smile he hoped would put him at ease, a smile that smacked of camaraderie, and leaned closer. "I know she told you to refuse me, but I really need to see her. Is there any way we can work this out?"

Tate sat back in his chair and met Richard's gaze. "Ms. Cruz isn't receiving visitors."

He put his hands up and took a step back. "Okay, I get it. She's your boss and I'm just someone you're supposed to keep out. Would you mind letting her know that I'm here? That way she can decide for herself whether or not to see me, and you stay out of trouble."

"Mr. Morgan, I can see that you really want this, but Ms. Cruz mentioned your name specifically when giving me my instructions. She will not see you. She was very clear on that matter, and I'm sorry, but I will not go against her wishes." Tate raised the receiver on his phone, his eyes never leaving Richard's, as though he were prepared to contact security.

"Then I'm very sorry to have to do this." Richard rushed past the desk, ignoring the look of confusion on the young man's face, and threw open Yvette's office door.

She whipped her head up then gasped, her eyes wide as he stood in the doorway. She looked guilty… trapped. Trapped by her betrayal, by her callous mistreatment of what they'd shared. When he'd arrived at Saffron, he was ready to forgive her on the spot, anything to get back to the way things were before. One thought of how she'd left him in the hospital, how she was so quick to use the situation to her advantage, and he couldn't let it go. Not here in the office where it all began, at least.

A confrontation had to happen; there was no way around it. Steeled against the emotions that threatened to derail his plan, an icy calm washed over him and he finally spoke. "You've avoided me and refused to talk about any of this, and I've indulged you, for the baby's sake, but now I'm done. We will have a child together, and only last week we were planning a life together. You don't get to simply flit off whenever it suits you."

She swallowed hard, but lifted her chin. "Maybe I'm done, too."

That was rich. He'd come to her to air their problems and forgive her so they could move on. "You can be done, if that's what you want, but today, right now, I need you to tell me why you left me at the hospital, mere hours after my father had a heart attack, without a word, without explanation." A bit of the anger faded, and his voice softened. "I think you owe me that much. We deserve that much."

"Fine." She said tightly, looking as miserable as he felt. "Come in and sit down."

He took a seat across the desk from her. "Why did you leave? Is this about my father?"

"Yes, I suppose it is."

His head dropped, and his shoulders fell. Hearing it confirmed shot through his gut. "I was afraid of that, but it doesn't make it any easier to take. You're not the woman I thought you were, the woman I'd hoped you were."

"*I'm* not the woman you thought I was?"

He ignored her, continuing on. "I guess there's not much left to do but decide how to proceed."

"How to proceed?" She sounded confused. Did she really think he would walk away from his child?

"I can't lie to you; this is bad. It hurts, worse than anything I can imagine. But I still want to be with you, to raise our child together. It'll take some time, but I will forgive you and we can move on."

She tipped her head back, her brows knitted together. "What the hell are you talking about? I don't need you to forgive me, because we're done."

"Wow. Well, even if you and I aren't together, we need a plan for how we're going to manage the custody of the baby. I still intend to be involved in his life, so we are most certainly not done."

"So that's it?" She asked, her temper finally piquing. "You want to make custody arrangements? Wow. You know, not so long ago, I thought we had a chance, that things had changed between us. I might have even thought we could fall in love." She scoffed, displaying the fire and fury that was missing earlier. "What a joke. Only you, Richard, could betray me, lie right to my face, and then simply discard the relationship without so much as an apology. I'm glad I uncovered your true colors when I did. Obviously, I saved myself a lot of heartache down the road."

His laugh was harsh, surprised. "What do you mean? I didn't betray you. You're the one who left when my father was too ill to negotiate a deal with you and your company. Once you figured out that I would be in charge, you knew that there was no way you'd make any headway on the merger."

"Is that what you think? Unbelievable!" Her voice rose, but she quickly caught herself and reverted to an unflappable professional persona. "You've got half of it right. I did leave you because you gained control of your company."

"I still can't believe it." He spit out the words, furious but wanting badly for it not to be true.

"I left because of *how* you gained control of Morgan Confectioners. I heard everything that night in the hospital, Richard—everything. I know why you proposed, and it makes me sick. Your father offered you control of the company if you got married, and you took the deal."

He felt the blood drain from his head, and for a moment he was speechless. "Oh God, Yvette, you don't have the whole story. That's not how it is at all. I can explain everything."

"What's to explain? Did your father offer you control of the company if you got married or not?"

"Yes." Richard almost whispered. Her face fell, and she tilted back in her chair.

"But that's not why I proposed! I never accepted his offer, and my feelings for you are genuine. I never considered using you to get what I wanted." He sat forward, wishing he could get closer but knowing she would rebuff him. "Yvette, I have been falling in love with you."

"You—" she paused, seething. "You have been lying to my face. To my face, Richard! Why did you even want me to stay here if you thought so little of me? If you thought I was the kind of person who would leave because I didn't get what I wanted in business?"

"Yes, I thought that you left for selfish reasons, but I put that aside for the sake of your health. Yours and the baby's. That's all I was thinking of."

"How very noble of you. You know, I thought my job was getting in the way of your heart's desire, that I was responsible for threatening your legacy. I felt horrible, like I shouldn't be doing it." Her voice cracked, and she swallowed hard. "Now I just feel like a fool."

"No, don't. You're not a fool. I am. I can't believe I let it go this far." He reached across the desk to touch her hand, but she snatched it away.

"Do you have any idea how difficult it was for me to let my feelings for you dictate what I did at work? I had to face losing the chance at becoming vice president for you, Richard. Vice president! But I almost did it for you, for your happiness." The anger was deflating from her voice, turning into sadness, finality. "All along, you knew it didn't matter what I did, and you just let me suffer. You let me worry about it, about you. Turns out you're just fine without me."

"I'm not, though. I'm so sorry about everything, and if I could take it back or do things differently I would." Richard shook his head. "I need you, Yvette. I need you in my life."

"I can't believe a word you say. Everything that we've shared in the last month has been a lie." Her eyes brimmed with unshed tears, but she held her head high.

"I know it sounds bad right now, but please, I'm begging you, let me explain." He pleaded with her, knowing he sounded desperate but unable to care.

"What is there to explain? Even if I could get past the deal you made with Michael, could believe that it had nothing to do with your proposal, am I supposed to be okay with the fact that you still thought so little of me that you believed I left you the night your father could have died because of something I had to do for work? I think that says more about you and your attachment to your precious company than anything about me. It's time you took a long look in the mirror, Richard. You really thought that my professional ambition was strong enough that nothing else mattered to me. If you think so little of me, why would you want me to stay?"

"I don't think I ever really believed that you left because of my father, it was just the easiest explanation. I think I was too afraid to face the possibility that you might not feel the same way about me, and I assumed the worst, that I'd been burned by someone who I'd cared about. Just like before." Her face was impassive, and there was nothing more he could add, no way to make it better. "If there's any way I can make this up to you, I'll do it. Anything."

"I don't know what would make this better. I really don't. This baby, the fact that I was able to get pregnant at all, is a miracle, and it's tainted with your betrayal. You've treated us like a business transaction, and that's why I have to go. I have to do what's best for the baby."

Her hand flew to her stomach, and he was immediately sorry for the confrontation, for the betrayal, everything. He rushed to her side and knelt beside her chair.

"Are you okay? I'm sorry, so sorry. I never meant for this to happen." He laid a hand over hers, only to have her jerk back as though she'd been burned.

"What more do you want from me, Richard?" She sounded defeated, bullied even. With rising concern, he took in the dark circles under her eyes, her waxy pale complexion, and sucked in a breath.

"What's wrong?"

She winced and quickly recovered her neutral expression. "I'm fine."

"You don't look fine." He took her hand, relieved that this time she let him.

At his touch, fat tears fell from her eyes, dripping onto her lap and darkening the purple fabric of her skirt. Yvette slumped over and shook her head. "Of course I'm not fine, Richard. None of this is fine." She grimaced and tensed up, sending an icy fear through him.

"What's happening?"

"Just cramping, a little nausea. I probably just need rest, and time alone." She sniffled and wiped tears from her cheek as she straightened her spine, appearing determined to appear strong again. "I'll be fine." She took a deep breath and visibly calmed herself.

"This doesn't sound fine. Let me take you to the doctor and get everything checked out. Then we'll know for sure." Suddenly nothing mattered but Yvette and the baby. Not the argument, not their relationship, nothing.

She winced again, this time not trying to minimize her pain. "Okay, I guess that won't hurt anything."

A uniformed security guard arrived at her office door, hands on his hips and a stern look on his face. "Is everything okay in here, Ms. Cruz?"

Richard stood and faced the security guard as Yvette waved her hand dismissively. "I'm fine, everything's fine. False alarm." She offered him a weak smile, and the officer narrowed his eyes.

"Do you need me to escort this gentleman from the premises?" The security guard widened his stance and straightened his back.

"No, it's fine. I'm sorry that Tate called you." She waved him away again before suddenly doubling over in pain. Her fingers dug into Richard's hand, and she looked up at him with panic in her eyes. "Can you take me to the doctor's office?" She uttered the last word through gritted teeth as she squeezed her eyes shut.

"Of course, let's go." He helped her to her feet, steadied her in his arms, and walked her to the door.

The guard stepped to the side, and she leaned on him as they rushed down the hall together.

...

Yvette sat up on the vinyl exam table and adjusted her clothes as she got comfortable. The paper liner rustled beneath her, and she moved her gaze to the sonogram monitor screen, the tiny counter holding tubes and jars, the poster on the wall. Anything to avoid making eye contact with Richard.

She'd let her guard slip in the rush of getting to her doctor's office, had let him care for her. She'd accepted his loving touches, his concerned eyes giving her port in the storm. The baby was fine, she was fine, and with the haze of panic lifting, she needed to reclaim her distance from him. Restoring the buffer of space between them was the only way she could guard against her feelings for him. Now was the time to remain strong, to forget how her heart leapt when he appeared in her office.

How had she been so stupid? So foolish as to think that he had turned around? Of course his feelings for her were and always had been motivated by his own selfish desires. He'd proposed to gain control of Morgan Confectioners and end her bid for acquisition, nothing more. Why had she let herself believe that their relationship could be real?

"Mrs. Cruz, it looks like everything is as it should be. The baby's heartbeat is strong, and everything looks good. I think you just had some round ligament pain, which can be frightening, but isn't dangerous. I'd like for you to get some light exercise and gentle stretches into your routine. That will go a long way towards keeping your body healthy." The doctor squeezed her ankles and legs, gently assessing for swelling. "Your blood pressure is a little high, but you don't have any serious swelling. That's something we'll need to keep an eye on. Pain and stress can increase blood pressure, and that's what I think happened today, but I do want you to be mindful and let me know if your symptoms persist or get worse."

"Okay." She swallowed hard before finding her voice. She'd let Richard Morgan have too much power over her, had given him too much influence in her life. Now that she had a baby to worry about, it was more important to insulate herself against him and the damage he caused. "Do you think this has anything to do with my radiation treatment? Is the pregnancy too fragile?"

"I think you can expect a normal pregnancy if you take care of yourself. Whoever told you that pregnancy after radiation was impossible was mistaken. Sometimes it can be more difficult to conceive, but obviously it's possible." He checked the chart in his hand. "Your bloodwork has all come back normal, and we don't have any reason to think that your pregnancy isn't healthy. However, if there's any way you can take more time to relax, especially this week, I'd do it. I'm not going to put you on bed rest just yet, but if things get too serious, that's what we're looking at next." He finally looked over to Richard. "Mr. Cruz, you can help a lot by making sure Yvette doesn't have too much to do or worry about once she gets home."

Mr. Cruz. She didn't correct him, but bile threatened to rise in her throat. Less than a month ago, she'd wanted nothing more than to become Richard's wife. Now the mere thought of pledging to spend her life with him turned her stomach. Seeing him nod and agree to care for her made her blood boil. How dare he? This was all his fault. All of it. He reached for her hand, a look of naked devotion on his face, and she snatched it away. No. Her terror at the thought of something going wrong with the pregnancy had distracted her into letting her defenses slip, but no more.

"Of course," he said, his voice deep, rich with rough emotion. "I'll do whatever I can to help."

"Great. Yvette, you can do all your normal activities, just take some more time for yourself. Let your husband do the dishes, try not to let trouble at work get to you, make sure you get enough water and rest, things like that."

If he referred to Richard as her husband again, she would lose it. She nodded, ready to get out of the office and away from both of them. Already, the thought of riding in the same car with him again was setting her teeth on edge.

"Thank you so much. I'll be more careful." She swung her legs over the side of the table, refusing Richard's silent offer to help her sit upright. He could play the part of doting husband and father-to-be in front of the doctor all he wanted.

"All right then. I'll see you at your next check-up. Just call the office if you have any questions or concerns." The doctor left, and she was left alone with Richard.

She could no longer stomach the charade, and wanted to leave. The sooner they got through the car ride back to her office, the better. Constantly reminding herself why she could never trust Richard again, why her feelings were a foolish mistake, was exhausting. Once he was out of her sight, she'd breathe easier. He'd never be fully off her radar, not with the baby as a constant reminder, but there were blissful moments when she forgot how she'd fallen for him, how she'd been sucked into the fantasy of building a life with him. Then it would come rushing back, all of it. The whirlwind romance, the perfect fit of home life with him, and the crushing betrayal.

• • •

Richard pulled out of the parking lot and stole a glance at Yvette before merging into traffic. She turned towards the window, refusing to look his way, a sheet of dark hair hiding the sliver of her face that he would have seen. Was she angry? Sad? Worried? Her hands clenched her handbag in her lap, and he watched as she tilted her face down. As painful as seeing tears fall would be, he wondered if it might be easier to get through to her if some of her anger dissipated.

With a resigned sigh, she pulled her cell phone out of the bag and tapped the screen. She turned her face towards the car window when her conversation began.

"Hey. Listen, I have a huge favor to ask. I'm leaving my doctor's office right now," she paused, listening. "No, no, everything's fine. Well, it will be. I was having some pain, and Richard took me in." Another pause. Apparently she'd told the other person about their break up. "My blood pressure was a little high, but other than that it seems okay. The doctor said it was probably just round ligament pain, but I need to manage my stress and limit my activities. I'm supposed to be able to go to work and do everything I need to do, but only if I take care of myself. Otherwise, I'll be put on bed rest, and that's the last thing I want."

Richard turned the radio off and adjusted the air conditioner vent. Yvette steadfastly refused to look his way, and he concentrated on his driving. It might not make much difference, but he'd give her no reason to think he was anything but helpful today.

"Yeah, so I was wondering if you could come and stay with me for a while." She laughed into the phone and tucked a strand of hair behind her ear. "No, I'm not trying to trick you into becoming my maid. I just need someone around to help me, to keep me sane. It could even be fun."

That vulnerability he'd glimpsed when she first announced the pregnancy was back, and it was heartbreaking. She should be joyfully planning for the arrival of their baby, maybe even making wedding arrangements. Instead she was begging someone, probably her sister, to stay with her so she didn't have any complications.

"Oh. Crap. Okay, no it's okay. I'll figure something out." She shifted in her seat and tugged the seatbelt away from her neck. "No, absolutely not. I haven't told them anything yet. I'll figure something out. Don't call them. Okay, I'll talk to you later. Bye." She ended her call and tucked the phone back in her bag.

"Was that Veronica?" He shot a quick glance at Yvette's profile.

She nodded. "Yes. I thought it might be better if I wasn't alone, so I could have help with regular household stuff and have someone there to look out for me. She's out of town for work, though."

"Come home with me." She scoffed, but he continued before she could interrupt or refuse. "You can have the bedroom to yourself. I'll stay in the guest room and will give you your space." They could hash out their unraveling relationship later. For now, she needed to focus on the baby.

"No, thank you."

"Listen, whatever you think of me, we can't let it affect your health or the pregnancy. I'll leave you completely alone if that's what you want. You won't have to see me at all, and that's a promise. Mrs. King will take care of you, and I'll feel so much better knowing that everything is okay with you and the baby."

"I'm sure Mrs. King has better things to do than babysit me, and the last thing I want to do is spend even a single night in that bedroom."

"Then take the guest room. Whatever makes you comfortable. Please, just think about it."

She was silent for several minutes, and Richard was too afraid to upset the relative peace with more conversation. Finally, Yvette set her bag on the floorboard and angled her body to face him. He turned to her for a quick look before returning his eyes to the road, just long enough to see the resignation on her face. "Fine." Her voice was stronger, clearer than he'd anticipated. "I'll take the guest room, and I expect you to keep your distance."

"Of course."

It wasn't what he wanted from her, but it was progress. That seemed like a good start.

Chapter Ten

Yvette let herself in and listened right inside the front door of Richard's house. After a few days of tiptoeing around him, she'd figured out when she could come and go without running into him at home. The house was quiet, so she dropped her keys on the table and kicked off her shoes. The cool marble of the foyer felt wonderful on her feet after being on them all day. With Mrs. King looking after her, she was doing less at home, but work wasn't slowing down a bit. Something had to give, or she'd be forced to give up accounts or worse, end up on bed rest.

She wandered through the quiet rooms, hating the tension she felt every time she saw a reminder of Richard. He'd given her the space she demanded, hadn't tried to talk her into reconciling once since she'd returned home, but it was clear that he was available when she was ready. He didn't avoid her like she did him. In fact, it seemed like he was eager to air their problems, ready to get everything out in the open. Strange, considering what he'd done. When they bumped into one another, he was calm, open, and ready to talk. It was as though now that he'd unburdened himself of the terrible secret, he was ready to hash things out and move on. She was the one who skulked around like a trespasser, locking herself in the guest room and sneaking out to go to work in the morning.

Holding her breath, she tried to slip past his office, hoping that it was Mrs. King she heard rustling around in there.

"Hey." His voice was soft. "You're home."

Clearing her throat, she straightened her back and summoned her willpower. That voice wouldn't melt her today. "Yes. I was just going to my room. See you later."

"Wait. We need to talk."

"I don't have anything to say to you."

He stood, hands on his desk with his head down, and paused for a moment before meeting her in the hallway.

"Yvette, please," she paused, hating the pull that the sound of her name on his lips still had over her. His hand landed gently on her shoulder and he moved in front of her to look her in the eyes. "What we've shared has changed me, has made me believe in love again. When I'm with you, I want to be a better person, and I believe for the first time ever that I can. I want you to be my wife, and I want us to be a family. I can't change what happened, but we can move forward. What we have together is special, and you can't deny that."

"What we had could have been special, but I think we're through. I'm sorry, Richard, but I don't think I can move forward. I can't take any more. I'm not angry, just sad. It's over."

She shifted, and Richard held up his hand. "Wait, let me show you something."

Yvette sighed, weary with the weight of her disappointment. Why prolong this? "What is it?"

A ghost of a smile pulled at the corners of his mouth, and disappeared as quickly as it came. "Come with me. Please."

Yvette followed him out of the office and through the house to one of the guest rooms, heavy with emotion and ready to see whatever it was so she could leave. The door to the master bedroom was open across the hall, and she looked in as they paused outside the guest room. So many memories lingered there. The late nights together, the beautiful conversations they shared, the amazing moments. Everything that made up her love for Richard started in the bedroom, where they were alone, cocooned in their own private world, and able to break down the walls they'd each built to keep others out. Not so long ago, that room was her sanctuary. Richard was her sanctuary. Now it was a bitter memory.

He pushed the door open and stepped inside, started to hold his hand out to her, but dropped it to his side. She edged past him, telling herself not to breathe in his scent but failing, and sucked in a breath. Hot tears welled in her eyes as her throat tightened.

"Do you like it?" He was so close, right behind her, but she couldn't face him.

She nodded, afraid she'd lose it if she spoke. The guest room was now a nursery…the most elegant, gorgeous nursery she'd ever seen. Richard thought of everything. The gleaming hardwood floors peeked out only on the edges of the huge plush grey rug dominating the room. An antiqued crib stood against the wall directly across from a matching armoire. He'd chosen grey and yellow bedding in a chic chevron pattern that matched the oversized rocking chair that sat in the corner. Hot tears trailed down her cheeks, and she wiped them away with the heel of her hand. Richard set a tentative hand at the small of her back, and she stiffened but didn't pull away.

"I can see you in this room, in that chair, or standing over there, looking into that crib. I see you everywhere in this house, but this room is us, together." His voice was thick with emotion, and something cracked inside her. He was too close, filling too much space.

"There is no us. Not anymore." The words came out almost a whisper, wavering. He wanted her to see this room as their future. All she saw were broken dreams and everything she'd lost.

"There has got to be a chance we can fix things. This can't be goodbye." He tried to take her hand, but circled her wrist with his fingers instead.

A small step to the side gave her the space to escape his touch. She sniffled and looked up at the delicate little crystal chandelier that filled the room with soft light. The chair would be perfect for spending hours holding the baby, feeding the baby, reading to the baby. She could picture it herself, and her heart squeezed with longing. That would never happen, though, because they were too broken now. There was a point in every relationship when things were stretched too much, pushed too far, to come back.

"It's time to move on." Her voice cracked, but there was no need to hide her sadness.

"I don't want to move on. I'm going to keep fighting for us." His voice was thick with emotion, with a sadness that told her he understood how serious she was.

It tore her apart that Richard wanted them to be a family so badly, but he still didn't get it. A baby between them didn't change everything. It didn't erase the fact that he'd proposed to cut her out of negotiations, and it didn't help her forget that at the first sign of trouble he'd assumed the worst of her. His first marriage had scarred him, certainly, but she wasn't the one who could heal him. Not if he didn't love her, respect her, and know her, and his knee jerk reaction to their misunderstanding showed her that he didn't. Not like he thought he did, and not like she deserved. She owed it to herself and the baby to provide stability. Living with a man who cared more for his company and legacy than a real marriage wasn't what they needed.

"I've got to go. I'll send someone for my things, and we'll discuss custody and visitation another time. Take care of yourself, Richard." She touched his arm lightly and spared him one sad look before leaving him alone in the nursery.

Chapter Eleven

"Thank you. I'll take care of him from here." Richard dismissed the orderly who stood behind his father's wheelchair. He offered his arm to his father as he rose, and nodded to the orderly as he wheeled the chair back into the hospital. When he refused assistance, Richard opened his car's passenger-side door for him instead. "Ready to get back to your own house?"

"Oh yeah. A few days in there seemed like an eternity. I can't wait to get a hot shower and to sleep in my own bed. Without a pushy nurse coming in every fifteen minutes to check my blood pressure." His father stretched and looked to the sky. "Looks like rain. That should make it easier to sleep."

His father slid into the passenger seat, and Richard made his way around the car. Outside the hospital, the sun struggled to shine through heavy, dark clouds. Traffic sped past on the nearby street. Life went on, it seemed. Heart attacks, broken hearts, none of it mattered. He put the car in gear with a quick glance at his father, and navigated out of the parking lot.

"Do you want to talk about it?" His father watched him as he drove.

Richard couldn't make himself look at his father, and kept his eyes trained on the road instead. "Talk about what?"

"You know about what. Yvette. Robert told me what happened, and I'm so sorry. I thought things were going well between you two." From the corner of his eye, he could see his father angle his body towards him, but he kept his eyes on the road.

Richard gripped the steering wheel tighter. "Well, it seems that things are over between us. She told me she wants to work out a custody and visitation agreement."

"Robert said that she left you that first night at the hospital, and that you think it had something to do with her not being able to negotiate with me anymore. You know, that doesn't sound right to me. Yvette's ambitious, but she's not ruthless."

"You're right, and I wish I had talked to you about it before I talked with her. Might have saved myself a lot of heartache." It was tough to admit that he'd doubted her so seriously, but perhaps his father could help him figure out how to make things right.

"So, what happened?" His tone was gentle, encouraging him to continue.

"She overheard the conversation you and I had in the hospital, and she knows that you offered me the company if I got married. That's why she left, because she thought I used her to get what I wanted. I finally came to my senses and figured out that I wanted to be with her regardless of what she'd done, so I confronted her, thinking we'd work it out. Things blew up, and I had to rush her to the doctor. God, Dad, I was scared she was going to lose the baby. It turned out that she was fine, just stressed and probably overworked. She only came back home with me because her doctor told her that she needed to take it easy or she'd have to go on bed rest. She wanted to go back to her own house, but her sister was out of town and she was the only one who could have stayed with her to help."

"Wait, what? You confronted her?" Michael scoffed. "How can you be so stupid about women?"

"In my defense, I didn't know that she knew about the offer. I was sick of the silent treatment, and I still thought that she was the one in the wrong. She wouldn't speak to me, and I was dying from the suspense." Remembering the confrontation turned his stomach.

"I'll assume that as soon as you figured it out, you got on your hands and knees and begged for forgiveness, right? So, how could it be over between you two?"

"She said that I treated her and the baby like a business transaction, that I hadn't changed, and that our relationship is too broken to go back. I'm at the end of my rope. I don't know what to do. We'll be in each other's lives because of the baby, but I don't know how it's going to work from here on out. I don't want to just share custody with her. I want a family. But, it's like now that the secret is out, it's going to be hanging between us forever. It could be forgiven, but not forgotten, you know? Even if she would forgive me, I still go to work every day. The buyout, your offer, all the problems, they're going to be like an elephant in the room."

"Sounds like you need to come up with a way to eliminate work being an obstacle."

"I know, but it's been such a huge sticking point for us the whole time." He pulled into his father's driveway and parked.

His unbuckled his seatbelt and slid to the edge of his seat, facing Richard. "Then obviously what you've been doing isn't working. Listen, you have to decide for yourself what you want. If you think you'll be content sharing custody with Yvette as you build your little empire, then by all means, carry on. If you want her, though, and a life with your family, you'll have to make that happen. If it's what you really want, you'll never forgive yourself for letting her go."

He frowned, contemplating a grim Yvette-less future. He couldn't bear it. He wouldn't. If she needed to see that he didn't view her or their baby as business, then he'd show her that.

"I think I know what I have to do." His father practically spelled it out for him, but Richard appreciated that he allowed him to reach the conclusion on his own. He could handle this, could make the grand gesture that Yvette would need to see how serious he was.

Richard helped his father into the house and left him in the hands of his capable and caring housekeeper before making a quick stop at his own house.

...

Soft music played from the speakers, rain pelted the windows as the sky darkened, and heavenly aromas wafted through the kitchen. The pouring rain outside gave the warm kitchen a cozy feeling, and for the first time in days, Yvette started to feel like herself again. Like everything would work out somehow, and she and the baby would be okay on their own. She stirred the sauce bubbling on the stove and smiled as the familiar scent of home drifted up from the pot. She brought a spoonful of sauce to her lips and blew across the top before taking a tiny taste.

"Perfect." She turned to her sister. "This tastes just like Mom's."

"Thanks. I've been working on it." Veronica peeked out the window through slats in the blinds and narrowed her eyes. "It's really coming down out there. Yikes."

Yvette glanced out the window and shrugged. "I like it. It's perfect weather for my life right now."

Veronica grinned. "Dramatic, much?" As she bustled around the kitchen, plating food, she shook her head in amusement.

"Don't make fun of me. You don't know what it's like." She kept her tone light, careful not to bring down the good mood they'd been sharing. It was too easy to slip into self-pity, to think about all that she'd lost. Richard's words stayed with her, how he'd begged her to stay, to reconsider. Not for the first time, she wondered if she'd been too quick to dismiss Richard's apologies, their relationship. She believed in forgiveness, in second chances, and she hadn't even considered it when he asked. She filled two glasses with ice water and followed Veronica to the kitchen table.

After setting the glasses at their seats, Yvette glanced out the picture window overlooking her backyard at the pouring rain. "Let me just grab a couple of candles in case the power goes out."

Stretching on her tiptoes, she reached for the carton of emergency candles on the top shelf of her pantry and patted her hand along the surface for the box of matches that was pushed back out of her view. The doorbell rang, and the box of matches fell from her tenuous grasp and bounced off her forehead and onto the floor.

"Can you see who that is?" She shouted to Veronica as she bent over to pick up the matches. She heard the front door open but couldn't hear who was there.

"Yvette?" Veronica called from the foyer.

"Coming!" She tucked the box of matches into the carton of candles and set them on the kitchen table.

The sound of heavy rain grew louder as Yvette rounded the corner to the foyer. Before she had time to wonder why Veronica had left the door open, she saw why. Richard stood in the doorway, his suit dotted with dark raindrops despite the umbrella dripping at his side.

"What are you doing here?" She wasn't prepared for the way her heart raced at the sight of him, or how tight her throat felt as she pushed the words out. For a moment, the rain, the music in the kitchen, everything faded away and Richard was the only thing she could see. Time stretched out, as though the space between them was thicker than the surrounding air.

"Can I come in? I need to talk to you." With his words, she snapped out of her daze and realized that he was standing inches away from the downpour.

"Of course. Come on in. I'll get you a towel." How long would it be before she could be herself, normal and composed, around him? Surely there would come a time when she wouldn't be so dumbstruck simply by sharing the same air. She had to believe that if they were to move forward, if they were going to parent a child together.

"I've got it. You two go ahead and talk. I'll make myself scarce." Veronica produced a towel for Richard and hurried off towards the back bedrooms of the house. Yvette had been so distracted by seeing him again that she didn't even notice her sister leaving in the first place. Whatever he was there to talk about, she needed to recover her wits. After everything they'd been through, all that he'd done, she still felt that magnetic pull towards Richard. How long would it be before she could see him without wanting to escape to his arms?

He dried himself off with the towel, and Yvette closed the door behind him. Drops of rain clung to his dark hair, dampening his neck and shirt collar. She stopped herself from reaching out and running her hand across the wet skin. "We can go to my library."

She led him through the house to the room where he'd proposed for the second time, the room where they shared the moment that she thought would change her life. Rain pelted the glass, and the clouds darkened the room, but her lavender stained glass lamps bathed the space in a soft light. The cozy atmosphere and the memories that surrounded them made her wish she'd chosen her home office for their meeting. But she was through with games, with jockeying for position, with treating her interactions with Richard like business transactions. All the careful planning that went into establishing a relationship with Morgan Confectioners is what got her involved with him in the first place. Letting her heart lead is what pushed her over the edge. He'd taken her through the gamut of emotions, had given her the best and worst moments of her life. Whatever he had to say tonight would be met without orchestrations or maneuvering. It was over, and she was tired. Tired and sad.

They settled onto the plush wingback chairs next to her bookshelves, and she pushed back the memory of the way her heart swelled the afternoon he'd proposed and she'd accepted. That afternoon seemed far away. The person she was that day seemed far away.

Richard ran his hands over his thighs and shifted in the chair. "So, I want you to know that I really listened to what you said the other night, and I understand where you're coming from. I really do, and I'm not just saying that." He cleared his throat. "Throughout our relationship, I've misunderstood you, I've jumped to conclusions, and I've projected my own problems onto you. I know that I've let my past influence me, and part of the reason I've been so quick to believe the worst is because it's safer than taking a risk on trusting something that's real, on losing something special. That's on me, though, and you shouldn't have to suffer because I didn't know a good thing when I had it."

"Thank you for that. I'm sure this isn't easy for you to say."

"It's nothing compared to the thought of losing you. I've been wracking my brain to come up with a way to make you see how much you mean to me, how little anything else means when you're not in my life. Without you, it's like I can't even breathe." He ran his fingers through his hair, and despite herself, she remembered how it felt beneath her own hands. "You felt like I treated the baby and our engagement like a business arrangement, that I used the situation to my advantage. As much as I'd like to deny it outright, it's at least partially true. I didn't mean for it to happen that way, but when I'm honest, I can see how I should have done things."

Being reminded of all the valid reasons they weren't a good match helped her shield herself from the growing warmth she was feeling for Richard. He was more vulnerable than before, more broken, even. She'd opened her heart to him, though, had sacrificed everything for their relationship, and he'd benefited from her loss. No apology, no matter how heartfelt, could remedy that without time. They couldn't be together unless he made some serious changes.

"I knew after you left that nothing I could say would convince you that I care for you more than anything else. There would always be part of you that doubted me, that still wondered whether or not I used you to get what I want. Yvette, there's a hole in my life now that you're gone, and nothing could replace you. Nothing. I don't want Morgan Confectioners if it costs me the love of my life. I don't want anything if I can't have you."

The love of his life? "What exactly are you saying?"

"I'm saying you can have it. You can have everything. If you want Morgan Confectioners for Saffron, take it. We'll get the paperwork started tomorrow morning. If you want to come and work with me in a true merger, let's do that. We'd love to have you join the family business, and just thinking about how far the two of us could go together blows my mind. But if you want to buy me out and give Saffron total control … or even if you just want me to shut the whole thing down, say the word. I'll do anything."

"I don't know what to say. Are you serious?"

"I've never been more serious in my life. My father and I agree on this, and he's on board … " He paused. "Although I hope you won't shut the whole thing down. No need to put all those good people out of work simply to prove a point." His mouth curved into a tentative smile. "But you don't have to decide right now—whatever you want." He stepped a little closer. "All I care about is you. All I want is you."

"You went to your dad?"

"Of course." His eyes glinted in the room's soft light. "I don't know anyone who's better at convincing beautiful women to marry him, do you?"

She laughed, and a single tear slid down her cheek. "No, I guess I don't."

"Without you, the house is so empty. I'm so empty. Nothing is the same without you there, and it's killing me. I don't want to go another moment without knowing that we will be a family. Tell me, please, that it's not too late for us."

"It's not too late," she whispered, her voice thick with emotion.

Richard eased off his chair and kneeled before her on one knee. "Third time's the charm, right?" His smile was boyish and hopeful, and her heart caught in her throat as he took a deep breath. He'd proposed to her twice already, but this time was different. This time, it meant something. He'd changed since they met, had become more humble, more open and real. "Sweetheart, when you first came into my life, I wanted you gone. I am so thankful that you stuck around to convince me that I was wrong. When you left me, my world stopped turning, and nothing was right with you gone. I can't imagine growing old without you, and I'll spend the rest of my life showing you how much I love you."

He pulled a small velvet box from his jacket's inner pocket and popped the lid open. As he plucked the ring from his cushion, her hands flew to her lips. He didn't hold the engagement ring she'd left behind. This one was smaller, more delicate, and it sparkled in the soft light of the room.

"This was my mother's ring, and it's one of the few things of hers I have left. My father gave it to me years ago so I could give it to my wife. You are the first woman who has ever meant enough to me to give it to, the only one I want to create a family with. I love you, and I want to spend the rest of my life with you. Yvette Cruz, will you marry me?"

Tears fell in earnest as she nodded her assent while he placed the ring on her finger.

"Yes," she whispered. "Of course I will."

Richard stood and pulled her to her feet along with him before wrapping her in his arms. With a hand cupped at the base of her head, he held her closer and kissed the top of her head. "I love you." His words were murmured against her lips as he tipped her face up to meet his, sending warmth winding through her body.

"And I love you." She fitted herself into his embrace, marveling again at how perfectly matched they were. Everything she'd ever wanted was finally right in front of her, and she couldn't wait to start a family and a life with the man she loved.

Epilogue

Saffron's newest venture, Millie's Candy Shoppe, was full of customers on opening day. Richard never would've believed that giving up control of the company he loved would make him so happy, but his wife had taken him up on his offer to put Morgan Confectioners under Saffron's control and ended up transforming it into something amazing. Between the research and development funding, the increased marketing, and the new family neighborhood store, the brand had flourished. Trading control of the company for the wife and child he'd always wanted was a bargain, and he hadn't regretted it for a minute.

Richard knelt beside his daughter, steadying her with a hand on her back.

"What do you think, Candace?" Scanning the row of old-fashioned bins of candy beside his toddler, his heart was full enough to burst.

"Pretty," she murmured, her big brown eyes wide with wonder. "Lollipop."

"Yes, baby, lollipop." He plucked a glossy pink confection from the bin and placed it in her chubby little hand, much to her delight.

Rising to his feet, he took in the atmosphere of the new store, grinning from ear to ear. The candy shop that meant so much to him as a boy was long gone, but this was a close second, and it felt like home. Yvette strode in, the door on the bell chiming behind her.

"Mommy!" Candace squealed, toddling to meet Yvette, who managed to avoid the sticky lollipop as she pulled her into a hug.

She dropped a kiss onto Richard's cheek and looked around, beaming. "It's really something, huh?"

Yvette had overseen every aspect of the store's development, from conception to completion, to be sure it was as close to the original Morgan store as possible. Framed black and white pictures of the Morgan family hung on the walls, the employee aprons were replicas of the originals, and for the grand opening, the prices were even the same as they'd been on the original store's opening day.

"It's perfect." He slung an arm over her shoulder and kissed the top of Candace's head, breathing in her sweet baby shampoo scent.

The young reporter covering the store's opening approached the family, handheld recorder ready to roll. "Mrs. Morgan? I've interviewed some shoppers and employees, so I'm ready for you whenever."

Yvette placed Candace in Richard's arms and led the reporter to a quieter corner so she could answer questions. He bounced his little girl in his arms, loving the sound of her giggle.

"Down, Daddy, down!" She squirmed in his arms, determined to gain her freedom.

With her feet back on the floor, she wandered around the bins again, enjoying her lollipop while she contemplated the array of colorful candies lining the row. Listening to the shoppers as he followed Candace, Richard knew the store was going to be a success. The neighborhood they'd chosen was perfect for the concept, and the people were looking for new family-friendly places to shop. His eyes fell on a picture of his mother, a huge smile on her face, standing in front of a big bin of colorful candies. She'd be glad to know that he'd found Yvette, would've adored Candace. Probably would've spoiled her rotten.

As he wandered, he'd made it to the corner where Yvette was finishing up her interview. The reporter held out the recorder. "One more thing and I think I've got everything I need. Saffron bought Morgan Confectioners, correct?" They nodded. "How did you ever convince the Morgans to agree to that?"

Richard scooped Candace up into his arms and answered for his wife. "Well, Yvette made me an offer I couldn't refuse." He winked. "Let's just say it was a sweet deal."

About the Author

Monica Tillery lives in Texas with her handsome husband and two sons, where she loves playing Bunco, reading, and hanging out with friends. She loves to hear from readers and can be found on Facebook at *www.facebook.com/monicatilleryauthor* or Twitter @ monicatillery. Check out the latest news and happenings at *www.monicatillery.com*.

More from This Author
(From *Adam's Ambition* by Monica Tillery)

Adam Whitman twirled his favorite Mont Blanc Starwalker in his fingers, enjoying the weight, and smiled to himself. This deal and the promotion that went along with it were as good as his. The partnership between Eco Initiatives and Everlight Optics would be the biggest contract he or anyone else at the company had ever brokered, and if he could just get the woman across from his desk to sign on the dotted line, it would be done.

"You're telling me you were a farmer? As in, you were out there in the field, picking tea leaves?" Christine Grazioli, Everlight Optic's CEO, shot him a suggestive smile from her spot on the sofa in his office.

He'd seen that look before, and if he played his cards right, the ink would be dry on the contract by noon. "I certainly did, from the time I could walk until the day I left home. My family owns the largest tea farm in Washington. You've probably had some yourself. Hold out your hand." He paused and picked up a crystal bowl on the table, holding it out to her. "Pick one."

She plucked a leaf from the bowl and handed it to him. He gave her a conspiratorial smile and turned the leaf over in his hand. "Nice choice. It says that an important decision you make will bring you much success." He dropped the leaf above her hand, letting it float gently into her open palm.

Christine laughed, throaty and seductive. "I don't think that's how tea leaf reading works. You're supposed to brew these and read what's left behind after I drink the tea." She glanced at her watch. "Oh, shoot. I've lost track of time. I need to get across town for a meeting at Paramount. Can we get in touch later?"

"Absolutely. I'll have the contract sent to your office; just send it back when you've reviewed everything and signed." He stood and opened the door. Once his client was safely down the hall, Adam fist-pumped the air in silent celebration. All it took was a nice working lunch and some harmless flirting, and he was on his way to closing a six-figure deal and locking in the promotion. This partnership would make the Eco Initiatives higher-ups very happy and guarantee him one fat end-of-year bonus. He laughed to himself; sometimes it was too easy. The tea leaves always did the trick. Women either believed in the magic or allowed themselves to think there was something between them. Who would have thought his upbringing on the family tea farm would still come in handy? He returned to his desk to review the paperwork so he'd be ready when she sealed the deal.

"Mr. Whitman, Richard Whitman is on line one." His assistant's disembodied voice came through the phone speaker, and he looked up from the proposal. How long had it been since he spoke with his father? Weeks at least. Far too long.

"Thank you, Lauren." Adam pressed a button on his phone and answered the call. "Hi, Dad." He sat back in his chair and relaxed, ready for a long chat. The deal with Everlight Optics would still be there when he finished with his family. He hadn't given them enough time lately. Or for the last several years, if he were to be honest with himself.

"Hey, son. Is now a good time?" The voice came through the line robust and hearty. It was good to hear him sounding so upbeat. They exchanged pleasantries until his father reached the real reason for his call. "I need you to come home."

Adam sat up straight. "What's wrong?" Fear gripped him and his blood ran icy in his veins. His father had asked him to come home once before, and only once. That time his mother's illness was taking a turn for the worse, and he had barely made it in time to say his goodbyes before she passed away.

His dad laughed. "Relax. Nothing's wrong. I'm looking to retire, and I could really use your help. Do you think you could get away for a week or two?"

A week or two? He would be lucky to make it through the weekend without getting a call about something. His job at Eco Initiatives left little time for any semblance of a normal life. When he wasn't busy with his own accounts, he was consulting on others or researching the latest technological advances in environmental sciences. His days were spent helping local L.A. businesses green their operations through technological improvements, training company sustainability officers, and consulting for lobby groups. He enjoyed working for Eco Initiatives so much, he rarely took vacation days and regularly worked sixty-hour weeks. Still, losing his mother taught him that he'd regret squandering his time when his family needed him. Once someone was gone, they were gone forever. If his father was asking him to come home, Adam knew better than to second-guess it. He never wanted to look back and wish he'd chosen differently.

"I could come up for a few days, probably. I don't know about a week." If his hunch was correct, his father wanted him to consider taking over the farm. His father had made no secret of the fact he wanted his eldest son to claim his place at the head of the family business, Emerald Tea Farm, to live out his legacy. He had heard it all his life and had resisted the pressure. His dad was getting older, and with no replacement in line, it might be more difficult to work it out this time. There was no chance that could be managed in a week.

"Adam, I need you, and I don't think we can wrap it up in a few days. I want to settle everything while I'm still able. I don't want to end up with a situation where I'm forced to hand everything over to the first willing body because I'm too old to do anything about it. Now will you come help me or not?" His voice was strong, determined.

"What about Chad and Daniel? What do they have to say about all this?" His younger brothers still lived in Emerald Springs and ran the family's other businesses. They would never come out and say it, but he always suspected they resented the assumption he would take over the farm, the family's lifeblood, when he was the one who left. Chad and Daniel remained loyal to the family in ways he simply hadn't, and they likely wondered why their father wanted Adam to come home so badly.

"Chad is busy with the restaurant, and Daniel has his hands full with the resort. They both say they're willing to help with the farm, but honestly I don't think either one of them has the time for it. They'd let the whole thing run into the ground before they'd admit they're not up for the job."

He laughed. His father was right; they would drop from exhaustion before they would ask him for help. "That's true, but what makes you think it'll do any good for me to be there?"

"Maybe you can talk some sense into them and help them realize they need to leave it to someone else, or maybe you'll come up with some way they can juggle everything. We might end up hiring someone to oversee operations, someone who doesn't have other businesses to worry about. That can only happen after we let the boys decide they can't do it, though. They'll never accept someone else if they don't get their fair shake first. Who knows? You might finally decide to join the family business."

His father rarely brought up the possibility of hiring an outsider to take over, and Adam took notice. If they were addressing the matter directly, Dad might finally be ready to retire for real—and had given up on Adam taking his place. He was surprised to feel the first twinges of disappointment and quickly dismissed them. He didn't want the farm. He had spent his entire childhood dreaming of leaving town and never picking tea again. He should welcome his father finally moving on, so why did it feel like something was being taken from him?

"I haven't worked in the fields in years, Dad. I don't know how much good I could do," Adam stalled.

"You know how little actual farming I do nowadays, right?" He could hear the smile in his father's voice. "I'm not exactly out picking tea."

"Yeah, I guess I can't remember the last time you really got your hands dirty." He sat back in his chair and stretched. "All right, Dad. I haven't taken vacation time in a while, and I suppose I can always work online if anything urgent comes up. I'll be there. I can probably swing five or six days." He clicked his mouse and scanned the calendar on his computer to be sure nothing pressing would keep him from visiting Emerald Springs.

"Thank you. This means a lot to me." Relief colored his father's tone.

"It's no big deal. Just give me a couple of days to get ready, and I'll be there. I'll let you know when I have a flight to Washington."

They ended the call, and he tapped his pen on his desk blotter, mentally calculating how much time he'd need before he could leave town with a relatively clear work schedule. The sooner he went to Emerald Springs and got everything squared away, the better. The nagging thought that his life wasn't tied up as neatly as he thought ate away at his confidence.

Over the past fifteen years, he'd held out hope his brothers would manage to work together to keep the farm in the family, but the other Whitman enterprises must be commanding too much of their attention. Daniel had always preferred the family resort, a perfect match for his attention to detail and appreciation for luxury, although Chad's work at the family restaurant was surprising, given that he excelled at the art of dodging responsibility. Adam had known tea farming since he could walk, and now he was in the position to take the company to another level. The farm had always been all-organic, but Richard couldn't fracture his focus enough to commit fully to both optimal farming and green operations. Adam could come in with fifteen years of education and experience and a fresh perspective, ready to revolutionize things.

He didn't actually want to leave his life and job in L.A., but now that he had time to dissect their conversation, Adam wondered why his father hadn't tried again to convince him to come aboard? It was probably best this way, best that his family held no unrealistic hopes or expectations of him. This way he could go home for a brief stay, do his part then get back to his life. So why did it feel like he was trying to convince himself? Could it be a small part of him longed for the life he always felt destined to live? No, surely not. He had worked tirelessly to create his new life; there was no way he longed for a return to the farm.

A senior partner stepped in from the hallway and rapped his knuckles on the doorjamb, interrupting his thoughts.

"Hey, Adam, you got a minute?" he asked.

He shut the browser window on his computer and stood, straightening his tie. "Sure, Mr. Campbell. Come on in. Can I get you a coffee or water?"

"Call me Mark, and no thank you, I'm fine. Please, sit." The partner came in and took a seat opposite him.

Adam sat but didn't relax as he waited for Mark to speak. He tried for an expression that said he was loose but confident. "I wanted to talk with you about your future at Eco Initiatives today. We've been watching you for a while, and you have an excellent record here. You're innovative, personable, and efficient. We appreciate your commitment to the environment and to the clients, and we feel that nobody else would be better suited for the position of accounts management for all of California."

He leaned back, ran his fingers through his hair, and blew out a long breath. "Wow. This is quite a surprise."

Mark laughed. "It shouldn't be. You've worked hard, and we think you're ready for the next level. Of course it comes with a lot more responsibility, but the compensation package will reflect that."

"I am flattered, really. This is an amazing opportunity. Would you give me a little while to think it over?" With this promotion, his dream job really, so close within his grasp, Emerald Springs seemed miles away. Strange how things could change so drastically. Just moments ago, he had almost allowed himself to consider taking over the farm.

Mark put his foot back on the floor and looked Adam in the eye. "Sure, of course. Take your time. I'll send over the details so you can see what you'd be getting yourself into, and you let me know what you think."

Adam stood as Mark did, and they shook hands. "Thank you, sir. I appreciate your faith in me."

"You earned it." Mark left, and Adam paced the length of his office, jingling change in his pocket, shocked by the news.

In the mood for more Crimson Romance?
Check out *Heal My Heart* by Elley Arden
at *CrimsonRomance.com*.